SWEET LOVE

SWEET LOVE

EROTIC FANASIES FOR COUPLES

Edited by

Violet Blue

Published in the United States, by Cleis Press Inc.,
2246 Sixth St., Berkeley, California 94710.

Printed in the United States.
Cover design: Scott Idleman
Cover photograph: Bruce Ayres/Getty Images
Text design: Frank Wiedemann
Cleis logo art: Juana Alicia

First Edition.
10 9 8 7 6 5 4 3 2

ISBN: 978-1-57344-381-4

For BLM

Contents

INTRODUCTION: SAYING YES

When you're in love, or at the very least about to fall in love, precariously perched over the heart's precipice, it seems that every question becomes a lover's question. What to wear? Should I…? How do I answer? Questions, and their answers, become charged no matter how innocent. He *will* see me again. She will see my socks. He will feel my mood. She will smell the perfume I choose, oh, so very closely. All my decisions are to be seen in the reflection of another's eyes.

It's exciting, thrilling, and life shared by two is indeed a thing worth having. It's also fun to share the experiences of reading and fantasizing. The first book I put together with couples in mind was *Sweet Life: Erotic Fantasies for Couples*, and its success attested to the existence of many couples who yearned for the sweet life and enjoyed the ideas and inspiration the book had to offer.

It's one thing to read a story to someone. It's another thing entirely to try one out. I've always aimed for my anthologies to be erudite literary erotica, as unforgettable as top-shelf character-driven fiction, but also suggesting fantasies so perfect they might be enacted in real life. But I hadn't yet found a person to do the thing I'd made obvious all along to myself and past lovers: to try it at home.

Until I was assembling this book.

Saying yes to your sexual fantasies, when you finally find yourself in that place, with an excited and willing play partner, is the most exciting thing you can do. You can trust me on this, as I now have experience taken directly from the pages of this book. You might say it has been road tested.

My ardent hope is that this book provides sexual inspiration and compels you to recognize love and sex in the complex characters as much as in your own life. The stories I've chosen are explicit, well thought out, cleverly crafted, and arousing as hell.

Trust me. I tried it at home.

Which story, I'll let you guess. But I'll tell you: the sexual experience I took from these pages and applied to my own romance, with all its trust and adventure, was like shining a light into two hearts and having it come back from the depths of a pool clear, bright, shining and true.

These stories illustrate why we're compelled to take the characters' sexual fantasies and make them our own. In the prolific Thomas Roche's "Clearing the Air," a woman finds herself in the position many of us do when faced with a sexy, slightly intimidating ex-girlfriend of our current beau: to be friends, or not? When she decides to "clear the air" between them, we learn new ways to refine our current lover's impressions of the one who came before. Renowned and compelling author Janine Ashbless takes us backstage in a daredevil act where the layered characters draw us in and make us hold our breaths as we anticipate what will happen if they "Jump or Fall" into their greatest sexual fantasies, and possibly love.

Accomplished novelist N. T. Morley opens our eyes to the possibilities of blindfolds and sexual fantasies as birthday presents in "Five Senses," a mesmerizing story about a woman in charge, a man with restricted senses and an evening out of his control, but entirely focused on pleasing his five senses. Accomplished erotic writer D. L. King takes the notion of "Her Turn" and turns it on its head when a sexy, slightly jaded peep show–booth worker gets home to her boyfriend and takes "her turn" while watching him in the shower.

Andrea Dale's "Storming the Castle," while lighthearted, does not disappoint for explicit sex, public risk and sexual fantasy, and pure storytelling. Kristina Wright delights and erotically delivers in her story "(S)pan(k)cakes": not just pancakes and a spanking, but a wonderful read that's a story fit for two—and a recipe to make your own, as the theme dictates.

In Emilie Paris's "Clothes Make the Man," the saying may be true, but panties make the leading lady squirm a little more when she's over her boyfriend's knee—and a surprise awaits a man who's come to expect a demure girl in Louboutins. Kat Black's shadowy and exciting entry, "Playing Rough," was difficult not to share before publication and leaves no detail of a very intense fantasy out: let's just say that parking garages might just enter your fantasy world in a surprising new way, as they have on this side of the editor's desk.

Kay Jaybee's "Searching for Her" distills the spirit of this book in a succinct tale of fantasies desired, abandoned and then at last discovered in a café—a kinky sexual adventure retold for our reading delight. "A Week and a Whip" is Allison Wonderland's entry into our lives, in which a woman seeks the help of girlfriends in understanding where her marriage went dry, with a solution as exciting as the title implies.

Felix D'Angelo is a regular in my anthologies and in my reading, and in "A Little Push" he does not disappoint. Here, we're pushed right into the action from word one, with a torrid anal sex encounter and a girl who wants more and gets it, with much happiness for her surprised boyfriend. It's also dripping with his trademark humor. When Jan Darby's female protagonist tires of her boyfriend's shortcomings (sexual and otherwise) in "Dishpan Hands," their relationship comes back to life in a way you likely won't expect: the "upper hand" indeed. And speaking of turnabouts, in Jude Mason's "My Turn," a woman's dominant mate decides he wants to experience what she does, and she more than rises to the occasion.

One of the names to watch for in erotica is Teresa Noelle Roberts, and she proves her mettle in the lyrical and very unusual story "Do You See What I Feel?" In it, a woman is bound in silky ropes and with her sweetheart's aid, is surrendered to a sightless dominant. "Better Bent Than Broken," by skillful Amanda Fox, playfully describes the range of a woman's response when discovery of her lover's secret porn stash reveals his longtime fantasy, one she isn't entirely comfortable with. But once she thinks about it and figures out how to make it hot and real for her husband, she relishes taking control, strapping it on, and driving him all the way home into orgasmic bliss for two.

How far can a fantasy go into the corners of our minds? As far as gets us off when we love and trust our partners, as revealed in the well-told story, "Safe," by Vanessa Vaughn. Here a woman experiences the night of her life—after thinking she'd bedded down at home alone, safe in her bed. Supremely skilled author Alison Tyler gives us an unforgettable serving of "Bachelor's Dessert," in which a woman gets distracted on her way home to her husband, giving in to a dirty, hard-edged sexual fantasy that has nothing and everything to do with him.

Filthy, hot and no holds barred is how I'd describe new author Dylan Reed's sublime piece of fiction, "Extreme Dogging." If you know what dogging is—public sex in cars, in view of strangers—then you have an inkling of how the story begins, but you'll never guess how it ends, with more than just a couple and a uniform thrown in for good measure. But it's the complex, very realistic and super-hot, "A Guy She's Never Met," by another favorite writer of mine, Zach Addams, that caps the tension and sweet release of the anthology. In it, a couple takes her number-one fantasy—him watching her have sex with a stranger—and gives it a modern twist, an unforgettable edge, and enough erotic inspiration to last the night (and beyond).

Take my advice. If you ever get a chance to try out your number-one fantasies—and I assure you, there will be more than one—in real life, say yes. It's well worth it. May this book, its adventurous authors, and the daring and satisfied characters, be your guiding inspiration.

You'll never get what you want unless you ask. And you'll never find satisfaction until you say, "Yes, I want it"—to yourselves, and to each other.

Violet Blue
San Francisco

CLEARING THE AIR

Thomas Roche

Audrey lay in bed nude and contemplated the problem at hand. It was serious, and getting seriouser. If she kept stewing, there'd be tension, and that just wouldn't be good hospitality. Audrey had been raised in the Midwest, where the host-houseguest relationship was considered as sacred as it was to the Greeks; eat your host's children or kidnap his wife, or, as a host, murder houseguests in their sleep, and you were pretty much screwed.

In that vein, letting things remain tense in this situation would be unthinkable, especially in light of this whole nonmonogamy, polyamory, whosama-whatsit weird processy thing. Weren't they supposed to talk everything through, ad infinitum, till the cows came home?

Nonmonogamy was Connor's idea, sure, but Audrey had gotten to like it. That was true even if neither of them had actually acted on it, and the promised threesome with a hot muscle stud had yet to materialize. She was as committed to this process as she was committed to Connor, and if there's one thing a dozen books on open relationships had taught her, it was that letting small problems fester turned them into big ones.

There was nothing to do but confront Kris. If nothing else, she needed to ensure that the next three days did not devolve into bitter innuendo and resentment, which at the moment they were sort of threatening to.

What had Audrey been thinking? An ex-girlfriend in the guest bedroom? Madness. But this was the naughties, goddamn it, and houseguests were houseguests.

Audrey stretched out in the slanted light coming through the venetian blinds; she could feel her body tingling all over, humming with anxiety and excitement. She rarely slept nude—and yet here she was, stripped and sprawled, horny as hell while still aching from the night before. She could feel the slick moisture between her legs, the hard press of her nipples against the soft cotton sheets. She could still feel Connor all wet deep inside of her, two of him, one face-to-face while he kissed her, the other from behind, her on her knees, facedown, ass up, legs spread and Connor pounding her, thumb in her butthole, hand in her hair, pulling hard as she squealed and came twice, not caring if Kris or the neighbors or the next county over heard her screaming obscenities, voice trembling with orgasm. She'd been much less concerned, at 2:10, whether Kris (or the neighbors) might hear her yowling "Please fuck me!" than she'd been, at 1:30, about whether they might hear her hissing "Don't make this about intimacy!" in a tone as accusatory as her moments-later "Yeah, pull my hair!" was conciliatory.

And here Audrey was, six hours later, naked, spread, wet, hard, panting, and still wanting more. She thought of her vibe in the top nightstand drawer—no, no time for that. She had to talk to Kris about what had happened last night.

Audrey bounded nude out of bed and went groping after her nightclothes; in a moment, she had squirmed into soft cotton shorts and a tight cotton T-shirt. Outside in the hall, she took long, slow, deep breaths, thinking, *Audrey, chill a bit—the girl's done nothing wrong. She's an ex, and Connor told you at the outset what good terms he was on with all his exes. Let's keep it that way—don't be the wife who fucked up all his friendships.*

So she did chill, creeping down the hall barefoot to the guest room, moving slowly and softly, and noting the door was ajar.

She knocked softly, said, "Kris?" meekly.

She pressed the door open, saw Kris's bright eyes come open, sleep-dull in that pretty face, beneath a rumpled mass of curly blonde that Audrey would have killed for—no, knock that off.

Connor was off at work, and would be till five; they had hours to kill, with those dumb girly plans for the Fine Arts Museum, shopping at Bonne Femme, lunch at La Méchante Salope, espresso afterward at Gusto Peccato, massages at Root Chakra and a trip to Audrey's favorite fag-hag hair salon, Tease de la Tarte.

If they didn't clear the air right away, the whole day would be agony.

"Hey, Kris, you awake yet?"

Kris stretched under the covers and brightened.

She squirmed up into a half-sit and said, "I am now."

She beckoned Audrey in, patting the side of the bed by way of suggesting she might sit down. Audrey did so, noting with some slight distress that Kris, either not expecting company or definitely expecting company, had left her vibrator on the nightstand. The device looked rather well used.

Audrey, sensing that her discomfort had already been spotted, tried to act casual.

"Oh, wow. One of those rechargeables. I've been thinking I want one." She guffawed uncomfortably.

"Well worth it," said Kris, smiling casually. She reached out, grabbed the vibe from its charger, switched it on, and pressed it into Audrey's hand with a wicked smile.

"The only way to fly," Kris said.

Audrey's face went hot in an instant; she looked down, flustered, as the vibe buzzed in her hand. Kris spotted her embarrassment, smiled and laughed, took the vibe away, put it back in its cradle. "Sorry," she said. "Didn't mean to embarrass you. I wasn't expecting company. I would have put it back in my bag if—"

"Listen, Kris," Audrey blurted, her face still red; her embarrassment had spurred her into action. "I've been wanting to talk to you.... Connor and I had a bit of a fight last night, and—"

Kris said, "Oh, really?" with a casual brightness that was not at all disingenuous but still made it clear that she'd heard it. Then she frowned and said, "I'm sorry, I'm a bad liar. I heard you fighting."

"I hope you didn't hear—"

"Didn't hear what?" This time Kris's poker face was much better, and Audrey was left wondering just how much she had heard. Audrey blushed deeper.

"Anyway...see, um, I'm just going to say it. We're trying out this new nonmonogamy thing."

"Connor mentioned."

Audrey caught herself gritting her teeth. She cleared her throat nervously, continued: "...So I'm probably a little oversensitive, but last night it, well...um...I'm not accusing, or anything, but it almost seemed, a little, I mean just a little, not really anything, but...um...should I let you, um, I didn't realize, should I let you get dressed? I didn't realize you were...um, should I let you get dressed or something?"

"Huh?" Kris had edged farther up in bed, into more of a sitting position, and the sheets had come sliding away; she was nude. *My god,* thought Audrey, *she has amazing fucking tits.* "Oh, I'm sorry—San Francisco. You know how we are out there." She covered up. "Sorry, didn't mean to embarrass you. Should I put something on?"

"Not at all," said Audrey, her eyes all but boring holes through Kris's hands and the sheet—*My god, were those real?* "Let's see," she said, flustered. "I'm not sure what I'm trying to say."

"You think I was flirting with Connor," said Kris. "You think I want to fuck him."

Audrey swallowed nervously.

"Bingo," she said grimly.

"I totally understand," said Kris. "I totally get why you'd be offended." She grabbed Audrey's hand and leaned forward again. Audrey's senses perked as she waited for the covers to fall once more, but the rules of physics seemed held momentarily in abeyance. Kris looked Audrey in the eye and spoke with enormous gravity. "I would *never* do anything to hurt either of you. I'm just kind of a flirt—I don't mean anything by it. I'm *not* after your man, Audrey. He's *yours.* Connor and I had a great time together, but that's over and it didn't work out and I'm totally into chicks."

Audrey stared.

"I'm sorry, did you say—"

Kris blinked innocently.

"Into chicks?"

"Women."

"Right."

"You're a lesbian."

"Bi. But—didn't he tell you?"

"No," said Audrey, breathing a sigh of relief. "That makes—"

She paused. She had been going to say something like, "That's a relief," but Jesus Christ, how fucking stupid would that have seemed?

Kris said: "Makes you more comfortable?"

"Oh, I wasn't uncomfortable," said Audrey, blushing, pulling her hands free and waving them madly, threatening to put an eye out.

Kris grabbed them insistently and held Audrey's hands firmly.

"Look, Audrey, even if I wasn't, I wouldn't be after Connor *at all*. Now he's found you, which is *totally* what should be. I think you're a *great* couple. Am I still attracted to him? Um, yeah, hello! How could any sane woman *not* want him? I mean, especially once she knows, you know, what he's *like*." She made a salacious little gesture with her eyes that looked far more filthy than if she'd grabbed her crotch. Furthermore, with each word she saw fit to emphasize—*never, totally, great, not, like*—her fingers moved not on Audrey's hand, which might have been affectionate, even sisterly, but rather on her wrist, kind of *up* her wrist, in a tingling suggestive caressing motion that made Audrey acutely aware that Kris was leaning closer.

"What he's like?"

"Don't play dumb," said Kris. "I was here last night. I have ears, Audrey. I'm sorry, I didn't mean to listen, but…it was a little hard to avoid." She looked guilty. "I tried to respect your privacy. I went out to make microwave popcorn, but—"

"We're out," said Audrey apologetically, pulling away. "I'll get some at Costco today—did you find the Doritos?"

Kris pulled her back.

"It's all right," she said warmly. "It really wasn't the popcorn…and anyway, I could hear you just as well in the kitchen. So I figured…" she shrugged. "Is that pervy of me?"

"You listened?"

"Only after you started enjoying yourself,

fight was…less interesting. Sorry."

"I'm embarrassed."

"Don't be."

"I'm mortified," said Audrey. She tried to pull away, but Kris wouldn't let her, which actually came as a huge relief. Audrey even let Kris pull her a little closer.

"Look," said Kris. "I know the nonmonogamy was Connor's idea. It was when he and I tried it, too…and it was rough going at first, but now I'm a true believer."

Audrey looked glum. "Believer in what?"

"Take your pick! Having more than one partner. Open relationships. Casual sex. Acknowledging when there's obvious heat between people. Allowing your partner to be horny, and sexual, and open, and have a good time and enjoy herself and express her sexuality. I'm a true believer in all of that."

Audrey breathed heavily. "I want to be, too. I want to be a true believer so badly."

"You will be," said Kris.

"But how?" Audrey frowned.

Kris looked deep into her eyes; Audrey could smell her, the soft musky night smell of a hot woman sleeping alone and naked after fucking herself with a vibrator. It was a good smell. Audrey was not entirely pleased that she liked it.

"You just do it," said Kris. "You know, seize opportunity. That's why it's nonmonogamy and not polyamory, at least as Connor conceives it. There's no negotiation up front—you sort it all out afterward."

"I don't think he'd put it that succinctly."

"Well…he's not the one who has a beautiful girl in his bed right now. Maybe I'm rationalizing."

Audrey's mind exploded with randomly collected thoughts as Kris inched closer, their eyes meeting between nervous smiles and the faintest sprinkling of laughter.

My god, Audrey thought. *Just the thought is so fucking filthy—his ex-girlfriend, and a houseguest. I couldn't. And I'm so not a lesbian. I mean, what does one even* do *with pussy? It's like...you can't put it in you. I mean, what would...fingers? Hm. Well, that's...and tongues. She's so pretty. I could never. I mean never.*

Besides, there's the interpersonal stuff. Out of the question. Audrey breathed deep. *She does smell quite good, though. Wow. She's not holding the covers very carefully. I can totally see half of her. My god, they're perfect.* Audrey's nipples stiffened.

"I'd love to be able to do that, Kris, but you don't understand. I was raised in the Midwest...."

"Right," said Kris, who had inched closer. "But you are in New York, now...and as an emissary from San Francisco, I feel it's my duty—"

Then it was over, and it was not a hypothetical should-we-start? the answer to which seemed murky at best, but a very concrete should-we-continue? which seemed pretty fucking obvious as a hot rush of excitement consumed Audrey's body.

Audrey never, ever kissed with morning breath—it was one of her rules, like the sleeping with clothes and the bulk-snacks-for-houseguests. She also was not a bisexual; all this college crap about girls making out to get frat boys popping boners right and left seemed like bullshit to her, and Connor's "everyone's bisexual" argument had been shut down by Audrey as the rank male hypocrisy it was, when she'd told him flat-out she'd eat pussy when he sucked dick.

Connor had shrugged. "Almost worth it," he said. "How about kissing?"

Sensing his annoyance and tacitly pleased by it, Audrey had leaned in close and said, "When *you* kiss a *boy*," with a saucy, naughty sound to it. Dismayed by her then-boyfriend's mischievous smirk, Audrey had spent the time between then and now vaguely anxious whenever she thought of it, because she found it vaguely terrifying, the thought of kissing a girl. If she did, she sometimes thought as she daydreamed, she'd like it to be perfect: a soft summer breeze blowing at a romantic nude picnic, say, with a string quartet playing "Just the Way You Are" and Catherine Zeta-Jones using stolen Russian plans or something to blackmail her into a make-out session. Such a thing seemed, at best, unlikely to happen any time soon.

But then, here Audrey was, about to make out with Kris, and she wasn't even drunk. Conditions were far from perfect, the interpersonal dynamics absolutely terrifying, and her lips still aching from hard kisses just last night from the man Kris had spent two years fucking. And here she was, trembling as Kris drew closer and their gazes locked, both bright with promise and fear. Audrey's tongue lolled out easily the moment they made contact, as if it was the most natural thing in the world not only to kiss her husband's slutty West Coast ex-girlfriend, but to do it open-mouthed with morning breath while drawing the covers away.

Floodgates opened, or at least it kinda felt like that, as Audrey surged forward kissing hard and pressed her cotton-clad body against Kris's naked one, bearing Kris back prone onto the bed and climbing atop her in an easy hands-and-knees posture in which Kris's slight, slim body fit easily under Audrey's taller muscular form. Their kiss deepened, and Audrey's body settled down as if of its own accord, her mind thinking so many thoughts at once that they all added up to thinking nothing at all. When one thought finally broke free, it was after Kris had gotten her hands up under Audrey's shirt and began to caress her back, easing up so far that just a few inches would bring those perfect hands with their pretty fingers into contact with Audrey's firm tits. And the thought that broke free was: *Am I being the aggressor, here?*

"Is this all right?" Audrey's thought spilled out between slurpy morning-breath kisses, barely audible with Kris's tongue half-stuffed in Audrey's mouth. She managed to pull back a bit to stare into Kris's quizzical look, and repeated her question: "Is this all right?" to which Kris rolled her eyes and made a *pfft* sound that said something like "Shut up and fuck me."

By then Kris had Audrey's shirt pulled up over her tits and was caressing her nipples with exquisite circles of her sweat-damp palms, so Audrey put up her arms and let Kris strip her down. The shorts were even easier; Audrey just felt Kris's legs going tight-wrapped around her, and one naked foot slid the thin cotton shorts to Audrey's ankles—and she surged forward, drunk with excitement, and pressed naked body to naked body, cunt meeting cunt so that Audrey cried out. Kris's was shaved, Audrey's trimmed close; with little between clit and clit, Audrey let out a long keening wail and her eyes rolled back into her head as she issued a long string of obscenities—not unlike the night before, when Kris had listened to Audrey spewing the same horny coprolalia, lying here spread with her vibe working rhythmically into her cunt.

That thought sizzled in Audrey's mind as her pussy went sliding easily against Kris's; had she seen this in a book or something? Watched it in a porno? It came so fucking easy; just tangle your legs around the other girl's lean back and—

"Fuck, that feels good," Audrey murmured, and Kris gave a cackle.

"Does it?"

Then Kris flipped her, the old creaky guest bed shuddering as

Audrey came down, legs spreading, head toward the foot. Kris pinned her with her hand tangled in Audrey's hair, and kissed hard. She then slurped her way down Audrey's naked front, tongue swirling around her nipples just long enough to elicit little gasps before heading south between Audrey's spread legs.

"Um...um...hey, isn't this wrong? I mean, Connor—"

Kris looked up wickedly from between Audrey's legs.

"Right. I'm sure he's going to be really pissed off that his wife and ex-girlfriend got it on in the guest bed while he was at work. I think he's really going to be upset about that."

"I see your point."

Audrey sighed as Kris's pretty face dipped down between her spread legs and her urgent tongue began licking Audrey's clit. Audrey's back arched and her knees cocked, her ass grinding hard against Kris's digging fingernails, the sharp pain mingling with the hot waves of pleasure from Kris's expert tongue. One hand wrenched free and traveled up to caress Audrey's tits. Audrey thought she was reaching up to hold hands or something—didn't lesbians do that?—and groped after them, but Kris's hand started caressing both her nipples at once, and Audrey's own hands went limp and helpless as she trembled all over. Kris's tongue swirled invitingly around Audrey's clit and down her cunt lips, teasing into the hole—oh, fuck, she was wet, she was totally wet, there was cum in there, filthy! Filthy! Filthy! Kris made a mewling sound, a sort of "Mmm, mmm," and Audrey, mortified, shut her eyes tight and tried to forget—*oh, fuck, fuck, this feels good.*

Kris, quite finished exploring and ready for business, settled into a rhythm. Her lips closed firmly around Audrey's clit, her tongue seething rhythmically. Audrey shut her eyes tight and rocked her hips against Kris's thrusts. She looked down at Kris, caressing the girl's hair, her arousal mounting as she watched

Kris get lost in the rapture of working her tongue against Audrey. Then two of Kris's fingers worked easily into Audrey's cunt. Kris kept her fingernails short—probably a lesbian thing—and Audrey felt the slickness of Connor's semen inside her, alternately thrilled and horrified by the feel of it dribbling out onto Kris's hand. Then she closed her eyes tight and forgot everything except the pressure of Kris's expert fingers on her G-spot and her tongue on Audrey's clit. But even so, she felt waves of anxiety—would she be able to come?

She felt the reach of Kris's arm over her, heard the click as the vibrator detached from the charging base; then she heard buzzing.

Mortified, Audrey opened her mouth to say, "Shouldn't you wash that?" and instead drizzled, "Oh fuck oh motherfuck oh fucking motherfuck oh fuck fucking motherfucking fuck fuck fuck fuck fuck," since by that time the dextrous Kris had gotten the tip of the vibe up against Audrey's clit, and now there was just no fucking question that anybody would ever fucking wash fucking anything, fucking ever again. Audrey clawed the sweaty bedsheets and thought up half a dozen new obscenities as Kris found exactly the right angle.

She was close, fast; her back arched and she leaned back screaming and clawing. Her arms went flailing over the edge of the bed, her eyes popping open, and—

Oh. That explained the footsteps.

"Um... Hi, baby," said Audrey.

"I guess you skipped the museum."

Funny how when you're doing one thing, you know, focused, you can hear a sound but not hear a sound, or not react to it. Shouldn't Kris have been paying more attention? *No, don't blame this on her,* thought Audrey. *This is totally you. You're the married one.*

Kris stopped licking, came up from between Audrey's legs with her face glistening and sticky. Her fingers were still thrust deep into Audrey, and both women could feel the pressure from Audrey's swelling G-spot.

"I can explain," said Audrey.

"I'm listening," said Connor.

"Hey, you're home early," said Audrey brightly.

"It's lunchtime," said Connor.

"Oh," said Audrey breathlessly. "Is it lunchtime already?"

"I see the two of you started without me."

"Free buffet," said Kris, clearing her throat. "Listen, Connor, do we need to process this for the next umpteen hours and get all weird, polyamorous blah blah blah blah on each other? Or would you like to fuck your wife?"

With that word, "fuck," Kris's fingers went gently pressing on Audrey's G-spot, and she gave a girlish little whimper, as if begging.

"I think I'd like to fuck my wife," said Connor, pulling off his tie and reaching for his belt.

"As I figured," sighed Kris as her wet mouth slowly descended between Audrey's spread cunt lips. "Like you haven't—oh, mm"—she made wet sounds, slurping whimpers—"at least thought of it?"

Then Audrey was lost in the taste and smell of her husband, as his cockhead nuzzled easily against her lips and went sliding deep into her mouth and then her throat—holy shit, this was a great position for that, throat nice and open, straight and relaxed. She had to pull back as she cried out and came, but besides that the only time Connor left her mouth was when he had all of his clothes off and was ready to fuck her.

To her credit, Kris asked nicely before she helped guide it in. And the little hot flare of jealousy that almost made Audrey say no was nothing compared to the surge of arousal as she felt Kris's perfect fingers not only guiding Connor's prick into her, but parting Audrey's cunt lips—holding her open, ready for Connor. Kris asked a second time before she kissed Connor as he fucked her; this time, Audrey didn't feel that hot flare of jealousy, just a pulse of arousal as she watched the two kiss above her.

Then Connor was fucking fast, and Audrey pulled Kris close as she came.

Afterward, they lay in a tangle for just about as long as it took for Connor to complain that he'd be late back from lunch. A nooner with two beautiful women, think the boss would buy this excuse?

Kris and Audrey kicked him out of bed; they had massages to get. And probably some talking to do, but not until after a rubdown. The day was still young—especially now that the air was clear.

JUMP OR FALL?

Janine Ashbless

Blayne is a locked box and I don't have the key.

He and I are clearing up on the set. We do it each night: every lightbulb, rope, link and socket has to be checked to make sure we're okay for tomorrow. The audience for *Jump or Fall?* has a lot of space to move around in; this venue was once a large shoe shop and half of the shelving is still there. That's a lot of places to dump crisp packets and unwanted leaflets—everyone's pockets are full of arts festival flyers—you can't walk ten yards up the Royal Mile without being mugged by a leafleteer—and we have to keep the place clean. It's in the contract.

From the corner of my vision I see him watching me as I push the broom around. I've got my long hair tied back in a single braid tonight, because I saw the light in his eye the first time I did it. The plait hangs like a rope between my shoulder blades. Most men prefer my hair loose—it's what they see first, it's what they remember about me—but Blayne is different. Blayne's so different I can't make sense of him at all.

Jump or Fall? is our theatrical art installation. I'm the theater, he's the art. I get to strike and hold the poses on the bar, the swing and the beam; I did a circus skills course just to make sure I was up to it. His pictures projected behind me are dark and vertiginous, deceptively realistic but emotionally engulfing. He's good. He's incredibly good. He's one of the most talented creative people I've met. We're already talking about our second project together, and we're definitely aiming for the Edinburgh Festival again next year.

I want him so fucking badly that my body is just one big ache.

The members of the audience walk around while the piece is in progress. They're supposed to, of course. They look at me from every angle, and depending on their standpoint they see me against one or another of Blayne's projected backdrops. I'm hanging upside down from the trapeze swing, my hands folded at my breast: am I asleep on a velvet bedspread, or diving from a high cliff, or a carcass in an abattoir rack? Am I relaxed or flying or dead? Context is everything; each position has meaning only when you know what's going on around it. A five-inch balance beam isn't frightening unless you're sixty stories above a city street. A woman kneeling with head bowed isn't alarming until she's doing it in front of a railway tunnel.

Every position I take is crafted to convey multiple stories depending from which angle I'm viewed. It's hard work holding motionless: I daren't lose focus. From the corners of my eyes I see the audience crossing and recrossing. When the pictures change I move, and new stories are recast.

Here's a story: I ask Blayne to a bar after the show and he agrees. Later we sneak past the guard of our Calvinist landlady into his room and fall into bed together. We fuck all night, and in the morning I'm so sore and blissed out I can hardly do the show.

But that story isn't visible from any angle, no matter how I turn.

He watches me, but he does nothing. He refuses to go drinking. He smiles when I smile, puts his arm around my shoulders without seeming to notice that it sends me into meltdown, plays with the ends of my hair—and then he walks away if the flirting gets too warm. I've never seen him lose his poise, which is extraordinary in this business. When things go wrong he just folds his arms and narrows his eyes and waits for it all to calm down or the solution to present itself. I've never met someone so self-contained, so reserved. I asked if he was a Buddhist and he just raised an eyebrow teasingly and shook his head. He's got eyebrows like flourished calligraphy and hair that's never tidy and lips pressed firmly shut over their secrets. He doesn't talk about himself. He's angular and thoughtful and I want to know if his cock's long and slim like the rest of him.

When it came to Blayne I fell, there's no denying it. Head over heels.

Tonight after I've swept up I climb onto the trapeze swing and idly watch him while he empties the bins, last job of the evening. Tying the bin-bag handles, he stretches.

"You coming then, Izzy?"

I roll off the bar and hang upside down, my feet hooked round the ropes. My braid hangs below me and I cast it back and forth with sweeps of my head, knowing he's watching. "Where are we going?"

"You fancy Thai tonight?"

"Hm. Dunno."

"What then?"

With a swing and a heave of my stomach muscles I pull myself back upright on the bar. He's wandered in closer. It's the plait, I'm sure. He has a thing for my plaited hair. I casually stroke the rippled length down my breast, wiggling the tuft at him. It's like fly-fishing: he walks onto the crash-mat, arms loosely folded, a funny little smile on his lips.

"How about sushi?" I ask, then drop and hang from the bar at the full extent of my arms. I'm wearing loose combat trousers and a white sleeveless singlet now that the show's over; the muscles are corded in my arms. My feet dangle well short of the mat.

"I thought you didn't like the idea of raw fish?" He's within arm's reach.

"Well." With one leg then the other I reach out and hook him round the torso, pulling myself tight up against him. "There's a first time for everything," say I with a grin. Hey, it's not subtle, but I've had it with being subtle. It was getting me nowhere. He looks up at me with surprise and doubt. Looks up, because his face is actually on a level with my boobs, which are straining against my white cotton top. I'm not wearing a bra and my nipples are hard.

"Izzy..."

"Hey?" I ask, softly.

With a certain inevitability his gaze falls from my face. I can hardly blame the man. Snaking an arm about me, he dips his head ever so slightly and his warm breath washes my right nipple. His lips graze the cotton and I stop breathing. He circles the raised nubbin of flesh with his mouth, establishing just how stiff it is, how thin the cotton covering, how warm and soft the mound of my breast. I feel teeth—the most delicate of exploratory nibbles—and I let out a squeak of anticipation and pleasure.

Instantly he lets me go and pulls out of my thighs' embrace. As he stalks away I drop to the mat.

"Blayne!"

He runs his hand through his hair and heads into the shadows. He keeps walking until he reaches a wall; I half expect him to just bump up against it like a toy robot but he leans his arm to the brickwork.

"Blayne, what's wrong?"

"Nothing."

"Have I pissed you off? Talk to me!"

"Izzy, please just forget it..." He can't meet my eyes, and his face is all pinched.

"Are you married? Gay?" I'm dead certain he's not gay, not judging by the way he's been watching me since we met. So certain in fact, that I reach out and grab the front of his loose trousers—and it's a good thing he has a hard-on because otherwise that would've been really embarrassing. He jumps when I grasp what is definitely a stiff cock, and a substantial one at that. "You are so not gay," I whisper, rather shocked at myself.

He could shove me off with one push, but instead he plucks my hand from his crotch and folds it against his chest, cradling it. His other hand takes hold of my shoulder. "Izzy, please."

"Have you got a wife then?" He doesn't wear a ring and I've never seen him with a woman, not once in months. He hasn't told me anything. "A girlfriend?"

"No."

"Then what's wrong?"

"Izzy, I really like you."

Oh, god: the poverty of the English language, where "I really like you" has to stand in place for everything from "I'm in love" to "I want to fuck your brains out" to "I want you to piss off and leave me alone."

"Then what's wrong?"

"I really like you," he repeats. "I think you're brilliant, and lovely, and great to work with, and what we've got going here is something so good. I don't want to lose that. I want us to be able to carry on together."

"Like I don't?"

"It won't work."

"I know something that thinks it will." I've already burned my bridges. "This big hard cock of yours thinks we'll do just fine together." I press against him to make my point, and he certainly makes his, right in the wall of my belly. My cunt flutters greedily. He shifts his hips, his eyes darkening. He's holding my hand really tight.

"Believe me," he says hoarsely, "it'll not work out right between us."

"Based on what?"

"Experience."

"Then just fuck me," I whisper. "I'm a big girl, you know: I can handle a one-night stand without going off the rails." I'm not playing fair either, pulling his hand from my bare shoulder down to cup the orb of my breast. He thumbs my nipple instinctively, sending electric flashes through my skin, and I moan.

"Izzy..." He sounds desperate, but he doesn't break. There's something weird going on here.

"Are you scared you'll hurt me?"

Something flickers in his eyes. "Far from it."

"Then what's the problem?"

He drags his hand from my tit and secures both of mine against his chest where I can't do anything naughty with them. I lean into him instead, my thighs burning against his. "Izzy, I have this thing..."

"I know. I can feel it."

He grins without any amusement. "There's this thing I do. It's...a part of my life. It doesn't come as an optional extra. And it's not something you'd be at all happy with."

"What?" For the first time doubt seeps in. "This is a sex thing, is it?"

"Yeah."

"Oh, god. Is it something illegal?"

He shakes his head. "No—consenting human adults only. I promise."

"But you think I'll freak out?"

"It's...difficult to understand."

"So you're kinky." I swallow, trying to be blasé. "I can handle that. I'm not a prude."

He pulls a face: disbelief.

"What is it? You like to wear women's underwear? Lick feet? Ah—it's not nappies is it?"

He laughs, and then shakes his head.

"Then what? What's so bad I won't even be able to work with you?"

"Can't we just leave it?"

"Too late for that."

He shuts his eyes for a moment. I feel something in the twitch of his muscles. I recognize it: the moment you decide to jump. "You ever been spanked, Izzy?"

"Oh," I say, all sorts of pieces sliding round in my mind, trying to find places to fit. "My first boyfriend—I sort of asked him to spank my bottom." To my own surprise I blush. "He called me a freak, and dumped me the next day."

"Ow." For a moment he's smiling again.

"Does that count then?"

"Um. It probably counts as a try."

"So...?"

"So: I'm into pain. In a big way."

"You want me to spank you?"

"Not receiving it. Inflicting it."

"Oh," I say again, wit deserting me. I've got enough sense left to realize that he's talking about more than a bit of playful ass-slapping. "Whoa. You get off on hurting people?"

"Women. Yes." He watches me wince.

"Don't you...?" I struggle to frame the question without sounding like a *Daily Mail* editorial. "Doesn't that worry you?"

"Worry me? Yes; all the time. I'm not a psycho, Izzy, or a wife-beater. I'm well aware of the responsibility."

For a long moment there's silence, while I stare at him and try to understand. Because it's still Blayne holding my hands there. He hasn't turned into some weird stranger. It's still Blayne with the anguished eyes and the twisted, rueful mouth, looking so good I want to eat him up. He doesn't have a moustache to twirl or mirror shades or a bloodstained hockey mask. He's the most grounded guy I've met. He doesn't lose his temper when frustrated or throw arty tantrums, even under provocation. He's the pinup boy for self-control.

Oh. Maybe that does make sense, in a way. And we're getting used to people admitting that they like being caned for kicks. I suppose for everyone who gets off on being whipped there has to be someone who wants to do the whipping. For every bottom there must be a top.

My lips are dry and I run my tongue around to moisten them. "You want to spank me, then, do you?"

He jerks his chin. "Oh, yes; I'd like to spank you. I'd like to put you over my knees and pull down your panties and spank your beautiful ass."

Oh, god. Oh, god. Where is this going? Why aren't I walking away right now? "Hard?"

He sighs. "Gently at first, until your cheeks glow pink. Then harder, as you warm up. I want to see you wriggle. I want to stroke your pussy and make you wet, so wet you're dripping on my hand and my legs, and then I want to spank you right there on your open pussy and make you squeal. I want to make you thrash about, and have to hold you down, and I want to keep going through your wildest struggles. I want to hear you sob and see your mascara streaked down your face with your tears. Do you get it now, Izzy?"

"Oh, god."

I get it now. I'm leaning up against this man while he holds my hands so I can't stop him doing anything, and I'm hearing him tell me in a low dreamy voice exactly why I should be scared of him.

And now that he's started, there's no stopping him. A steely look creeps into his eyes; he's seeing himself without flinching and showing me too. "I want to rope you up and slap your pussy and your tits, Izzy. I want to whip you. I want to pinch your nipples until you beg me for mercy. I want to hold you close and see the fear in your eyes and smell the sweat of your pain, and I want to know you trust me to take you through that clear to the other side."

He hesitates, a hitch in his throat.

"I want to be there when all the barriers go down, Izzy; when there's no faking or trying, just your raw naked need. I want to make you come over and over without being able to control yourself, in the middle of everything you dread. I want to inflict unbearable delight. I want to take you places you don't dare go to on your own, and I want to carry you through the dark and hold you and comfort you and kiss the tears away and make you whole again."

He lets go of my hands. There's a bleak and haunted look on him as he sets me on my feet, like a man saying good-bye.

"So now you know."

"Shit."

"Yeah."

How do you react when someone you like tells you he wants to hurt you? That he gets pleasure from your pain? We don't like such people, do we? We hate and fear them. Since I was little I had, like most girls, run away from hurt. We don't get into fights, we don't ride our bikes down steps just to see what happens, we don't skin our knees and get up and keep going.

"Okay," I admit. "That scares the hell out of me."

He nods. Told you so.

I put my hand on the wall, because my legs feel wobbly and my body's quivering. I want to feel something solid to lean on. The painted bricks are cold on my bare shoulder. Blayne turns as I do, so we're face-to-face, still close as lovers. It's the intimacy of confession. "It turns me on, too," I whisper.

His eyes widen slightly, but what I read there is doubt and concern. He lifts his hand to my face and traces his fingers down my cheek.

"Just listening to you talk makes me..." I swallow hard. "Wet. I'm all wet." My knickers are sodden, my pussy swollen and heavy. But, amazingly, he shakes his head.

"I'm not trying to convert you, Izzy. It's something you either get or you don't."

"I do get it. I think. A bit. The pain thing..." I'm trying to think past the tender, regretful caress of his fingers. "When I had my tattoo done, it was horrible for the first five minutes. I had to force myself to stay put. And then this endorphin rush kicked in I guess—and forty minutes later it was still hurting but I just wanted it never to stop. Pain's...a weird thing."

"Complicated," he agrees. "More so than we're ever told." He smiles. "I didn't even know you had a tattoo."

"Want to see it?"

He nods. "Please." I think I glimpse then how vulnerable he is in his need, and how isolated. How he must hold himself on the edge, waiting for permission to jump. I turn my face to the wall, pulling up the clingy cotton of my top to expose my lower spine and slipping the top button of my trousers to drop them low on my hips. It's a barbed tribal-style tattoo at the small of my back, nothing very original I suppose, but I love it. The delta of black thorns is like a magical ward over the cleft of my bum.

Blayne touches the ink and I shiver all over. Then he slides to his knees behind me. I feel the first touch of his lips and I'm flying, my heart pounding in my chest, my head full of the beat of wings. The tip of his tongue follows, warm and moist, tracing the path of the tattoo. I hear his soft groan. My fingers feel clumsy, but I manage to slip three more fly buttons and there is cool air on my cheeks as my trousers fall away to expose the curves of my out-thrust rear.

He can't resist that, can he? My bottom, offered to him as a gift, tied in the lace ribbons of my very tiny thong?

No, he can't resist.

His hands cover the twin globes of my ass, warm on my cool flesh. Then with a surge he's standing again, pressing into me from behind, squashing my breasts to the brick wall and grinding into me with a cock so hard and imperious that he seems likely to split the fabric of his own pants. He grips the rope of my braid and slowly tugs my head back, and with the other hand he delves under the jut of my ass, between my thighs, scrabbling aside the elastic lace of my gusset. Finding wet. So much wet.

"You weren't lying, were you?" he breathes in my ear.

I whimper, words fleeing as he explores every whorl and hollow and swell of my sex. Blayne growls under his breath, a bass line to the soft high noises I'm making.

"What's your safeword, Izzy?"

Off the top of my head: "Trapeze."

"Good." He pulls away—but not to release me: his hand whips through the air and lands with a stinging slap on my butt. I feel the wobble and the shock runs up and down my spine, right to the tips of my toes. Adrenaline crashes through my system, looking for an outlet: anger or panic. I push away both, gasping, and ride the burn.

"Feel free to cry out," he whispers. He wraps my plait round his fist and tugs at my scalp, and there's something about that small but specific pain that brings tears to my eyes and makes my breasts tingle. "Ask me to go slow or fast. You can beg if you like: it won't stop me. But I will take it easy…this first time."

He pulls away from the wall. He's got me by the hair; I have to follow, my ankles hobbled by my fallen trousers, every tiny step. He takes it slowly, savoring the way I hang from his hand. He turns me into the crook of his arm. That's the first time he kisses me, right there, with his fist in my hair and my head pulled back and my throat exposed. And here's the weird thing: he isn't rough—though his grip in my hair is unrelenting. He's sweet and soft and sensual. He holds me close, supporting me as much as pinning me. He whispers my name as we break for air, both breathing hard.

I touch his face. I've wanted to touch him for so long.

Another tug on my hair. My breath catches in my throat and I know my eyes flash hurt because I see it reflected in his expression and I feel the surge of his cock.

He lets me go. He walks away backward, step by step, and it's like I'm seeing him fall from me. He takes one of the chairs set out for the audience to rest in, the type with the orange plastic seat and the metal legs that squeal on the lino tiles, and sets it in place: *squeal.* Then he sits, his thighs apart. He pats his left one; an invitation. His erection is making a tent of the cloth over his groin.

Funny: I'd assumed that cruelty went hand in hand with being rough. I'm learning all sorts today. He's asking me to join him. To jump.

Here's the thing. When I was doing my circus training I'd had to learn to stop fleeing pain and failure. Looking over the edge of the trapeze platform at a bar hanging in space, hauling myself up a rope ladder yet again with my shoulders burning—it wasn't easy for me. That little girl inside had called the shots for so many years. Cowardice was a constant temptation, and it took me time to learn that I could ignore it, to build my strength, to take the risk. To accept the pain, because only by pushing through it would I reach what lay on the other side.

I kick off my shoes and trousers and walk across the cold lino. A little clumsily, I settle myself across his knee. It's not comfortable, and I strain to keep my head up. I wonder why he wants me over one thigh, not his whole lap.

Then he slides his hand up my spine, pushing me firmly face-down, off balance, and he catches one of my knees under his other leg to stop me tipping onto the floor. I hear the purr of his flies being unzipped, but I can only picture the way his cock springs free. So that answers that question, anyway. My ass is staring at the ceiling, my damp gusset exposed to the cool air. He strokes me lovingly, making me quiver, then he pulls my panties down to my thighs and then he hits me.

Slap, it goes on my ass; *KABOOM* it goes in my head. I gasp. The sting and shock are followed by an exquisite burn—and then another blow.

Thank god he does go slow: I don't think I could have handled it otherwise. He's actually being a lot gentler than his avid description, but it's my first time and I'm not sure what I can take and my head is full of fear and questions and weird old shame left from childhood and outraged pride. I'm struggling desperately for some kind of mental control; it takes a long time for him to persuade me to let go because though my legs are dangling over the abyss I'm still clinging to the safety barrier in my head. His patience is saintly. He uses both hands, his fingers dancing over my sex between each slap, delving into the hot wet places, comforting my hurt, persuading me to trust him, to surrender, to take more. My ass starts to burn and throb, swollen with racing blood. With each blow I long for his caress, and then with each caress I long for the next blow. He makes me forget everything: my dignity, my reserve, my fears. My self.

I don't burst into tears, not this time: he's not that harsh on me. But I do squeal, over and over again, especially when I'm coming. Then I scream like a seabird in flight.

The hurt is gone, just like that, even though he's still slapping me. In the no-gravity of orgasm, pain is pleasure.

The moment I start to come down he tips me back off his knee onto the floor between his splayed thighs. I'm looking up at him and clinging to him and I'm flushed and gasping and he looks...awestruck and proud. Yes. We kiss, clumsily. I try and squint over my shoulder to see if my bum really is the bright red balloon it feels like. He strokes my hair and my face and I smell my own wild scent on the fingers he's had inside me. I reach for his cock: it's standing up from the gash of his open flies, a solid column of need, smooth and dark like wood that's been polished with handling. I can smell myself on his cock too; he's been stroking himself with the hand laved in my cunt-juices. When I've got my breath back, I promise myself, I'm going to suck that cock—but for the moment I'm all a-wobble with shock and orgasm.

"Please tell me you packed a rubber when you decided to jump me," Blayne groans.

I nod.

"Good." His voice is a low ache. "Because I need to fuck you, Izzy."

So I go on hands and knees to get the packet from my discarded trousers. I crawl not because I have to, but because I want to: I want him to see my scarlet ass, my wet, inviting split. And when I crawl back I smooth the latex skin down his hot hard length with my mouth as well as my hands. Greedy Izzy wants his cock, so bad.

"Oh," says Blayne to himself. His belt is already uncinched; he draws it out through the loops and wraps the leather strap about his right hand, leaving the last six inches hanging like a tongue. I stop sucking dick and lift my face, the old nervousness reappearing in a flash. "Lick it," he whispers.

So I take the leather tongue in my mouth and suck it wet. I think he nearly loses control just there, but he clenches his teeth and holds back. Blayne is his own master.

And mine, just now.

His hand is in my hair again. He uses my braid like a leash to take me on hands and knees across to the crash-mat, and the tug brings tears to my eyes; I'm scrabbling to keep up. Then he sets me on all fours on the plastic-covered foam and mounts me from behind, driving his cock deep into the hole I have wet and waiting for him. Oh, god, I'm stretched tight. With every thrust he snaps that six-inch strap on my spread cheeks, and it's like being licked with a tongue of fire. I squeal in protest, my ass bucking, but it doesn't make any difference. My front end collapses to the cushioning mat; I thrust one hand back between my legs and grab my clit for dear life.

And that's how he fucks me the first time: riding me from behind, yanking my head back by my braided hair, whipping my buttcheeks with his belt. I've never been made love to with such exquisite care, such minute judgment. And every fucking second

I think it's too much, that I can't take it, that I'm going to call a halt—in a moment—only that moment never comes.

Instead, oh, dear god, I do. And then he does too.

Jump or Fall?

Jump!

FIVE SENSES

N. T. Morley

I hear the door creak open. Then I hear footsteps, a mix of bare feet and, I suppose, high-heeled shoes on the carpet of our living room. I keep my hands pressed firmly on either side of me, the velveteen couch soft against them. I take a deep breath and smell a mingled bouquet of perfumes and female bodies. I look into the darkness and listen for the next cue.

The first thing I feel are lips against mine, kissing me. One tender, soft kiss, its taste familiar, the brush of your smooth cheek against mine, your fingertips tracing a path down my chest to the top of my boxer shorts. Then you're gone, and I feel another kiss, someone else's, the unfamiliar taste of a new woman, her tongue grazing my lips very gently. Her hand caresses my cheek, then my neck. Then there's another kiss, from someone new, someone more aggressive with her tongue, forcing it deep into my mouth, kissing me hungrily, her teeth nipping my lower lip. Then two more kisses in rapid succession, one on my lips while someone else licks my ear with the tip of her tongue. I don't know whether to count four or five, and I suppose it doesn't matter, because I'll never know.

The music starts, slow and sensual, chilled trance with a dark, erotic feel. I sense a body near me, then I feel her thighs on either side of mine as she climbs onto me.

Her breasts, naked, brush my face, their firm nipples teasing my lips gently apart. She dances in time with the music, her fingers stroking my face as she grinds on top of me. Slowly, she lowers herself into my lap and I feel the press of her pussy, through my boxer shorts and what feels like a G-string, against my crotch. My cock stretches hard against the shorts.

The music grows louder, rising in intensity. The woman atop me dances more vigorously, her body rocking back and forth as she presses her crotch to mine. I hear whispering, distantly, mixed in with the music, and a faint spray of giggles. There are five of you, total, I'm sure of it.

Then I feel someone leaning over the back of the couch, feel a kiss on the side of my neck. I take a deep breath and smell you just as the woman dancing for me leans forward, and I hear—or perhaps sense—the two of you kissing.

She reaches down and touches my cock, gently stroking it through the thin, damp fabric of my boxer shorts. Her fingers close tight around it, gently kneading my shaft.

Then again—maybe they're your fingers. That's the beautiful, terrifying part. I'll never, ever know.

"Lap dancing is sexy," I told you. "There's something really erotic about not being able to touch."

"But you can still see everything," you said.

"Yes, you can...see, smell, feel with the rest of your body. You can hear her breathing, hear her talking to you. You can even taste her."

"Taste *her?*"

"Well," I said. "Sometimes they kiss."

"Not in clubs," you told me. "Do they kiss you in clubs?"

"Not usually," I said. "But sometimes, if they're breaking the rules. And they want a big tip."

"Is that hot?"

"Incredibly."

"And if you weren't in a club—say, if a woman was dancing for you at home?"

"With the same rules?"

"Well," you smirked. "I think if it was at home you'd be allowed to taste a little more. But not touch."

I smiled. "Yes," I said. "I think that would be hot."

"Would it be hot even if you couldn't see? If you were, say, blindfolded?"

"Yes," I said. "I think that would be incredibly hot."

"Because then you'd have *to use all of your five senses?"*

I laughed. "Four," I said. "I'd only have four senses."

And you smiled at me, looking mischievous, exceptionally naughty.

"No, you'd have five. Because you could imagine how good she looked on top of you."

"Yes," I said. "I guess I could."

"I know you love to let your imagination run wild," you said, caressing my face. "I think that would be the ultimate thing for you. Being lap-danced by more than one woman, say, never knowing which was touching you at any one time. Maybe never even knowing who they were, what they looked like."

I looked at you suspiciously. "Why?" I asked you.

"Well," you smiled coquettishly. "You do *have a birthday coming up...."*

* * *

She turns around in my lap, spreading her legs and sitting down on my cock. I can feel the strap of her G-string against the shaft of my cock. She grinds her smooth, full buttocks against me, wiggling her ass back and forth in time with the music.

The way she's stroking me with her ass feels more incredible than I could have dreamed. She leans back against me, her back naked against my bare chest, her shoulders rubbing my face. Her skin drapes over me, curtaining my face in the scent of her. She reaches back and caresses my face. I hear her breathing heavily as she rocks against me, her soft sighs rising in time with the music.

I hear whispers, giggles. Apparently this first dancer is hogging all the fun.

She lifts herself off of me, and I feel another body against mine. Her breasts brush my face again. This one is wearing a lace top, her breasts fuller and heavier than the other. The lace feels rough against my lips, especially with her nipples stretching it so taut. She smells different, floral, more perfumed. I feel the press of heavier fabric against my cock, hear the creak of leather; she's wearing a leather G-string, possibly, or maybe leather hot pants.

She lifts up her lace top and brushes her naked tits over my face. I breathe deeply of her scent, let my lips part slightly, let my tongue laze out to taste her flesh. She's salty but somehow sweet. She pushes her nipple between my lips and I suckle it gently as she grinds her crotch down onto mine. I'm moaning softly, the sound muffled by her nipple. As she bends forward I don't feel her hair at first; as she rubs the top of her head over my face, I feel that she's got short hair, cropped in what must be a cute little pixie cut. Is it your friend Shauna, I wonder, or is it some dancer you've hired for the evening? Would a dancer let me suckle her breasts like this? Would Shauna? Then I feel the hot pants grinding hard against me, her pussy deep inside them, and I remember how sexy Shauna looked in her little leather outfit that one time we all got dolled up for dancing. She squirms on top of me and I feel her upper body, bare against mine as she rubs the lace shirt over my face. I inhale deeply of her scent. She slips the lace away and discards it. Her lips press against mine and I feel her tongue working its way into my mouth; in that instant, I let it go, not caring whether it's Shauna or a complete stranger, a college girl making two hundred dollars an hour. I only care that her tongue is warm, slick, soft in my mouth. And that her breasts, now naked, are gently brushing my chest, her nipples hard and inviting so that when she slides up my body and moves them into my mouth, they feel better against my tongue than anything I could have wanted.

When she eases herself off of me, I feel the caress of gentle fingers down my front, sliding into my boxer shorts and wrapping around my cock, stroking it. That must be you, mustn't it? You would never let another woman, friend or stripper, touch my cock directly—would you? But when I feel lips against mine, taste the salt of a woman's tongue, I know it's not you—the way she kisses is different, entirely, than the way you do it. As she strokes my cock she dances in time with the music, rubbing against me. She's wearing nothing but a crop-top she's pulled up over her breasts, and when she slips her hand out of my shorts and sits in my crotch, legs spread, I can feel the moistness of her naked pussy rubbing up and down against my cock through my boxer shorts. I hear myself moaning uncontrollably; the touch of a naked pussy, even through the cotton of my shorts, feels so good I'm afraid I'm going to come. She sits down hard in my crotch, firmly wiggling her ass back and forth as she leans back and reaches to caress my face, her long hair sweeping across my shoulders. It's so long I can feel it down my chest, almost reaching her ass. Monique, I wonder? Your friend from the office, who you once made out with at a bar after work? I inhale deeply, smelling the faint hint of hibiscus shampoo, the barest suggestion of sharp, musky feminine sweat. She moves in time with the music and I want to reach down, slip my cock out of my shorts, and slide into her. Except that those aren't the rules, and I would never break them—because then this torment would end, and it's the most delicious torment I've ever known, a torment for all my five senses.

Monique—or whoever—rises off of me and I feel another woman climbing into my lap, this one smaller, with very slight breasts she uses to tease my lips. Her nipples are very large and extremely hard, and it excites me to taste the new taste, so very slightly different from the last woman. I imagine her, cataloging your address book of adventurous friends—and knowing, all the while, that I probably don't know her. Is she beautiful, I wonder? It doesn't matter, because the touch of her nipples on my mouth is electric, sending a surge to my cock, and I'm quite clear that however beautiful she is, I'll never know it. I suckle on her nipples gently as she settles down on me, rubbing her crotch against mine. She's wearing shorts, possibly spandex, but they're so skintight that I can feel the lips of her pussy against my cock, even through the boxer shorts. I smell her and detect the aroma of sandalwood, lost in a mix of feminine lust and the sharp scent of pussy. She swings around and sits in my lap, facing out, her ass slim and slight against my cock. She reaches back and parts her cheeks gently so she can slide my cock between them, the head popping free of my boxers to stroke her through the spandex. When she leans back, grinding in time with the music, I feel her hair, curly and long, caressing my face. It smells faintly of the smoke of clove cigarettes, sweet and exotic, and when she rises off of me, I miss it.

Then there's another body on mine, unfamiliar. I smell sex, hard and sharp in the sweat-heated room. The woman kisses me, hard, her tongue plunging inside me, her ample breasts tight against my chest, nipples hard. She grinds her crotch against mine, and she's so wet that I feel the front of my boxers soaking through. She's naked—fully naked, not guarded by any of the scraps of fabric that each of my previous tormenters wore. She kisses me harder than you do, more insistent, more unforgiving. She tastes so salty it's almost like blood, and she smells so sharply of sex any other perfume would be lost. When she reaches into my boxers and wraps her hand around my cock, she grips it hard enough to almost make me come.

But she knows men's bodies well enough to keep me from climaxing, and she deftly slips my cock out through the fly of my boxers. What she does then shocks me.

I feel her pussy enveloping the head of my cock. Surely she's teasing, isn't she? You would never let another woman fuck me. Or would you?

Then she sits down, hard, forcing my cock deep inside her.

She moans so loud I recognize the voice immediately. She grinds her hips on top of me, pushing my cock up hard against the depths of her cunt. She wraps her arms around me and pulls me closer, her lips finding mine and her tongue delving deep into my mouth. She starts fucking me with a fury, a desperation, a passion you've never shown. She's fucking me for *her* pleasure, and if I come inside her it's only incidental. Her sighs and moans mount quickly toward a peak.

I think I'm going to hold back, to let her come first. But I don't, because she comes so fast it surprises me when she grabs me and clenches me tight against her. Her body goes rigid for an instant, her hips immobilized in the explosion of pleasure. Then she's fucking me again, her body sliding up and down the shaft of my cock, juice dribbling out and soaking my boxers. It's only an instant more before I come, my ass lifting off the sofa, my mouth open in a cry of ecstasy.

She kisses my face all over, familiar kisses as I breathe a familiar smell. Why I didn't recognize it at first, I don't know—except that the five of you, or four, or six, or seven—had awakened my five senses so much that I smelled new things in the familiar aroma of your pussy.

When you rise off of me, I feel my cock slick with my come and your pussy. You sigh, whisper to me to keep the blindfold on. I hear whispers, giggling voices. Familiar, unfamiliar—who knows? With so many senses, I'm bewitched and misled at every opportunity.

I hear footsteps as you all leave the room. It's only when I've heard the door close that I take a deep breath and pull off the blindfold. I squint into the light.

The dancers' clothes, all of them, shoes included, rest discarded in a pile on the coffee table. When they walked out of this room, they were all naked—leaving me to wonder. Did I really recognize the sound of your moans, the feel of your pussy, the explosion of your orgasm? Or was it another woman who made love to me, as you watched, as you directed her, enjoying the sight of me lost in the oblivion of five senses?

That's the beautiful part, you see.

Because I'll never, ever know.

HER TURN

D. L. King

Lauren held her palm up to her mouth and slowly licked the first three fingers before starting at the top of her left breast and running them down and over the taut nipple. She skipped over most of her torso, making contact with her flesh again just under her navel. She looked out at the dark glass in front of her, tilted her head, letting her straight brown hair cascade down the side of her pale body, and smiled. She knew he was there and just on the edge of coming. The same guy had been feeding token after token into her meter; god knew how much he'd already spent, she wasn't keeping track, but this was her last window. Her shift was ending.

The fingers moved steadily down her shaved mound to the very top of her slit. She opened her folds with two fingers and let her middle finger touch her clit, which was already erect and protruding. She heard a muted gasp. She also heard the movement of the chain as the metal wall began to slide down, covering the dark window. The way the booth was lit, she couldn't see out, but she could hear her audience.

"No! No no nonononono... Fuck!"

Lauren got up to leave as Irina, her replacement, entered the booth and the metal partition, once again, rose on its chains.

"What? No. Wait! Wait a minute. Oh, fuck, oh, man..."

Lauren looked back at the glass and blew a kiss, then wiggled her fingers in a farewell wave before she stepped out, her long hair swinging, and closed the door behind her.

She'd started doing sex work when she was in grad school. She'd danced topless and stripped and made some very good money. Her student loan balance was extremely manageable and she'd been able to pay her living expenses without a problem. Now that she was almost finished with her dissertation for her doctorate in human sexuality, she was thinking that she might miss sex work, or at least this kind of sex work. As a sex therapist, she figured she'd still have her hand in, so to speak.

She'd been working the afternoon shift, from noon to four thirty, and she was getting hungry. She planned to get home about six o'clock. Sal, her boyfriend, would already be there. Maybe they'd go out for dinner after. After they'd gotten cleaned up and de-stressed from their separate workdays. Or maybe he'd cook.

Sal was gorgeous. He was six feet of muscled, Italian beefcake. A trader by day, he was her private gourmet chef by night. He'd been taking Saturday classes at one of the city's best culinary institutes because he preferred a kitchen to the exchange floor. He practiced on her. As soon as he had his culinary degree, he planned to quit the market and open a little Italian restaurant downtown. He had everything it took to be successful; business sense, looks, and real talent in the kitchen. He also had his restaurant nest egg stashed safely away for just the right time. Yep, he was a great Italian cook, but right now Lauren knew what she'd prefer to slather in his special red sauce, and it wasn't cannelloni. Work always made her horny.

It was a bit of a commute to the apartment she and Sal shared. It was one of those unbelievable new places, across the river. She'd never have been able to afford anything like this, but together they were doing all right. Actually, Sal paid the lion's share of the rent, but as he kept saying, she'd be supporting him once she completed her degree and started charging a couple hundred bucks an hour as a sex therapist.

When they'd been apartment hunting, it had been the bathroom that had sold her on the place. It was big and luxurious. Her last apartment's bathroom had been out in the hall. It wasn't like she'd had to share it, or anything. It was just that you had to actually go out the front door of the apartment and open another door to get into the bathroom. It wasn't all that uncommon, and she'd gotten used to it, but it was so small you could barely turn around, and there was only the one tiny window in the shower and that faced a brick wall.

This bathroom had both a soaking tub and a glass-enclosed shower. It had a vanity area with two sinks, beautiful modern fixtures and opulent tiling. There was a big, picture window over the tub, so you could look out over the river, toward Manhattan, while you were soaking. The room was light and airy and she would have spent all her time in it if Sal had let her.

The selling point for him, of course, had been the kitchen. And quite a kitchen it was. It was big and open to the living space. It had a Bosch dishwasher and a Kitchen Aid refrigerator and a Viking range. It seemed he had the same affinity to the kitchen that she had to the bathroom and she practically had to drag him out of it more often than not. The apartment was a wet dream come true. Heaven forbid they should ever break up. She didn't think she could go back to living in some hole on East 83rd Street again.

When she got to the building's entrance she checked her

watch. It was just six o'clock. Sal should be home by now and waiting for her. Taking the elevator up to the fifteenth floor, she very quietly let herself into their apartment. She made her way into the bedroom and took her shoes off. Leaving her jeans and sweatshirt in a pile on the floor, she quietly entered the dark bathroom, wearing only a pair of black satin tanga panties.

Sal had closed the blinds to block out any ambient city light and had turned off the main bathroom light. The only light in the room was in the ceiling of the glassed-in shower itself, and it was focused on the naked body presently occupying that space.

Lauren took a seat on the towel bench against the far wall, facing the shower. Once she had closed the door, the bench, and most of the bathroom, became cloaked in shadows. She leaned against the wall and spread her legs.

The light in the shower's ceiling was like a spotlight on Sal's naked body. She watched as he ran his soapy hands down his chest. He circled his nipples and pinched them slowly. As the water sluiced down, straightening the hair on his chest, Lauren watched his cock react to the attention he'd paid to his nipples.

He added more soap to his big hands and leaned his head back, closing his eyes. He soaped his neck, bringing his hands back down his chest again, this time circling and teasing his nipples with his fingers. His hands continued on to his navel, but instead of wrapping around his cock, they circled toward the back of his body and his ass.

Lauren's breath caught. She let one hand snake down, inside her panties, while the other teased one of her nipples. Sal turned around, facing away from her, and bent over, giving her a good view of his ass. As he spread his legs, she could see his full balls, hanging low between his legs. With more soap on his hands, he soaped the globes of his bottom and slipped them into the crack. While he ran them slowly up and down the split between his cheeks, Lauren ran her index finger up and down the now-slick folds of her own sex.

He inserted his hands into the crack and pulled his asscheeks apart, exposing his opening to her. She heard him groan. She was groaning quietly too as she dipped a finger inside herself while holding her labia open. She watched the water run down between his asscheeks while he slowly stroked and rimmed his hole with a finger before letting go of his flesh. His hands disappeared for a moment, returning again freshly soaped. This time he reached between his legs and soaped his balls, slowly stroking and squeezing them while the soapsuds ran down his legs.

Lauren moved her foot from the floor and brought it up onto the bench, next to her bottom, while she bent her knee away from her body, opening herself wider. By the time he turned around to face her again, she had two fingers buried to the second knuckle. Seeing the state of his hard cock, she groaned softly and began to pump her fingers in and out of her wet pussy, grazing her clit just enough to bring her to the edge of coming and keep her there.

With soapy hands, Sal wrapped a fist around his cock while his other hand automatically went for his balls. As he began to slowly stroke his cock, he broke the third wall of the performance and looked directly at Lauren. As their eyes met, a thrill of electricity shot through her brain, directly to her clit. Her fingers stilled and, not letting her eyes lose contact with his, her body bucked out its orgasm.

After it was over, she stripped off her underwear and stood on slightly shaky legs. "Hi, baby, how was your day? Mind if I share that shower with you?"

She slowly advanced on him, the slightly exaggerated sway of her hips driving him crazy. Stepping inside and letting the hot water beat down on her head, she grasped Sal's erect cock with one hand, and wrapped her other arm around his waist, hugging him to her. "Your turn," she said. Their mouths met as her thumb brushed lightly over the head of his cock.

STORMING THE CASTLE

Andrea Dale

It still astonished me that they were going to destroy it.

I stood in the twilight, watching the shadows deepen around the crumbling stone walls and dark empty windows of the castle ruins. Through the shattered courtyard archway I could see the first pinpricks of stars, tiny glittering lights against the blue black sky.

At this magical hour, I could believe almost anything. I could imagine a ghostly figure gliding along with a guttering torch, hear the clomp of hooves and jingle of harnesses over where the stables would have been.

The one thing I needed to believe was the only thing I couldn't: that we'd save Pencraig from the developers.

"Cassidy, come on!" Joe shouted from the car, impatience clear in his voice. "I want to get to the pub before they run out of crumble like they did last night."

Little could stand between Joe and the demands of his stomach.

I slumped down in the seat as he turned the car around on the rutted excuse for a drive. There was no sense talking; he knew what I was brooding about and he felt the same—he was just more pragmatic about it. We'd been through it again and again over the past three days we'd worked there. Nothing left to say.

Nothing left to do.

The car bounced down the narrow lane toward the main road. I left my window open, breathing in the magnolia-scented, soft summer air.

Maybe Joe was right. Maybe we should give up, let go. Shower off the grime and the weariness of three days of fruitless digging, get a good hot meal (complete with apple-blackberry crumble, which did sound awfully good), write up our archeological report in the morning.

They'd sent us here because they were sure the place had already been picked clean. We were there only as a formality, so that some faceless person could rubber-stamp a piece of paper that would serve as Pencraig's death knell.

The new owner couldn't tear down the fortified manor house, but he had plans to develop the area around it: golf course, luxury hotel, the works. The castle itself would be a ruined curiosity—a modern ancient folly, if you will.

I glanced over at Joe, seeing his profile against the flash of headlights on the A-road: a strong, handsome curve of brow and nose and chin. Unbidden tears pricked my eyes.

It wasn't just about Pencraig that I felt failure.

I let Joe shower first, and as I stepped in he was heading down to order himself a lager and me a cider and to make sure they saved us some crumble. I tried to tell myself I was bone-weary and suffering from low blood sugar, and that after supper I would feel less tragic.

But I also knew I was lying to myself.

I'd met Joe at university when we were both studying archeology. Our mutual interest in our field brought us together, and by the time we'd graduated, we were a couple. We got jobs together with the government and had been living together for six months.

And I was bored, bored, bored.

I loved Joe. That's what made it so damn hard. I loved him and respected him. We fit well together at work and at home, with similar interests and habits. Everyone thought we were perfect for each other, and I was hard-pressed to come up with a good reason why we weren't. It was just that the spark was gone.

Frowning, I scrubbed shampoo into my hair (Joe called it pixielike, and he loved ruffling the short dark locks with his fingertips). I was smart enough to know about New Relationship Energy, savvy enough to understand that you wouldn't have the drive to act like crazed love-monkeys forever.

I just felt like we'd never really been like that.

Sex was pleasurable, sex was good. Joe was attentive, making sure I came at least once before he did. Wackily enough, that might just be the problem. He was so concerned about it, so focused. We never had that wild, abandoned thing that you see in movies: swiping everything off the desk, breaking dishes on the kitchen counter, fucking against the wall with most of your clothes still on because you can't be bothered to take them off.

God, I was getting horny just thinking about it.

My soapy hands were on my breasts almost before I realized it—small, pert breasts, but I was inordinately pleased with my nipples, large, dark swollen peaks that were wonderfully sensitive. With slick fingers I pinched the buds, feeling the tug all the way down my body, through my belly to my groin.

I couldn't imagine how women could have their nipples

pierced. If they were as sensitive as I was, it must be excruciating. Still, I had a curious fascination with what nipple clips must feel like.... Nothing too sharp, of course.... My fingernails were short by necessity for my job, but I grazed them across my flesh as best I could.

The tremors shook me to my core. I'd forgotten that I could get aroused so quickly. I wanted a lover who could do that to me—and who needed me as fast as I needed him. I didn't need lather on my hand to slide my fingertips over my clit. I was wet enough down there, thank you very much, not from water but from my own juices.

I propped one foot on the edge of the tub for better access. Tepid water sluiced across my skin—the problem with being the second person to the shower—as I closed my eyes and let my fantasies run free.

A rough lover. Oh, let's face it, a Tudor lord, home from the War of the Roses, desperate with longing for his lover. The manor house of Pencraig stood on the foundations of earlier fortifications; this lord would have had the money to build that grand structure for his lady love. He took her now, though, without thought to the future; without thought, only with desperate longing.

Stripping her out of her dress, he'd loosen her corset and fill his hands and mouth with her breasts, the pleasure almost as much his as it was hers. He wanted to please her, but he needed to touch her for himself, too.

Undergarments abandoned, he'd fling her onto the bed and feast on her, filling his senses with the taste and smell and feel of her. She wouldn't be scented with deodorant soap, but neither would care. Her pungent scent, his sweat-salty skin would be part of their desire, mixed with the lavender and rose she used to sweeten her clothes.

Or maybe that was the smell of the expensive spa soap I'd brought with me, my one indulgence when I traveled.

That Tudor lord, he'd gasp and shudder when his lady wrapped slender fingers around his cock, so close to the edge from wanting her that he almost couldn't contain himself. Gritting his teeth, he'd turn her away from him, and she'd barely have time to clutch the carved headboard before he plowed into her tight heat from behind.

Grasping her hips, he'd fuck her until she screamed and her convulsions sent him to the edge and beyond.

The fanciful vision worked its magic on me, too. My clit jumped and pulsed, and I shoved two fingers inside of myself, coaxing my orgasm to go on just a little longer, oh, yes, just like that.

I staggered out of the shower, knees weak, and threw on clothes: cargo pants, faded Queen T-shirt, no bra necessary. I swiped a towel against my hair, and I was done. Joe would be wondering what was taking me so damn long.

Ah, the irony of that. I wouldn't be surprised if he wondered that on a regular basis.

Biting my lip, I trotted down the close stairs. Had I answered my own question? Was it time to let go of Joe, accept that our relationship had as much depth as the archeological dig we'd just done—which had revealed nothing of worth?

The apple-blackberry crumble was fantastic, tart fruit and sweet crunchy topping smothered in hot custard. At this point, it was the highlight of my sorry day. (The orgasm in the shower had been good but served as a reminder of everything that was wrong in my life.)

It was probably two a.m. when I crept out of bed. Joe never stirred. The B&B room contained one of those faux double beds, really two twins shoved together. He'd never been much of a cuddler anyway. I shucked on my clothes, left a scribbled note on my pillow, and was out the door without hearing so much as a break in his snoring.

Out the door and on the road to Pencraig.

I didn't know why I was going, I really didn't. It's not like I could dig something up under the moonlight, or stumble across some unique architectural feature that everyone else had completely missed, but which would bring the development process to a screeching halt because we'd have to research and catalogue it in depth.

I guess I just wasn't quite ready to give up. Or maybe the opposite was true: I had to find in myself the strength to say good-bye.

We had several flashlights in the trunk with the rest of our gear, heavy bright Maglites for peering into dark places, and I grabbed one before heading toward the manor house.

Some call the night still, but I say they aren't listening hard enough. A breeze rustled through the brambled hedges and overgrown trees, and the faint squeak of an unfortunate tiny creature was followed by the low hoot of an owl carrying supper to its lair.

The air itself felt alive. I didn't believe in ghosts, not really, but by the same token, when I dug up an artifact, it wasn't a cold, emotionless object to me. It had belonged to someone once. Someone who lived, loved, cried, dreamed, and died. I felt that everywhere I worked—that people's stories were embedded in the walls, soaked into the stones and earth and combs and buckles and horse-straps and cooking pots.

As I walked through Pencraig, carefully because most of the flooring had rotted away years ago, I found myself imagining the inhabitants as I had in the shower. Not just the lord and his lady wife, but the children, the scullery maids, the grooms, the chatelain and master of the hawks.

To make money between school terms, I'd done tours at various historic sites. My talks always got rave reviews because, attendees said, I made history come alive for them. I told stories about the people who'd lived there, weaving in facts and dates to enhance the tales rather than overwhelm them.

Here at Pencraig, had the master of hawks pined for the forbidden love of one of the stable boys? Had a cook's assistant longed for the touch of the lord's brother? Had the chatelain and the children's nursemaid had a torrid, lustful marriage, marred only by the babies that died before they took their first breath?

All that and more, through generations.

I pulled my faded gray jumper more tightly around my shoulders and stepped back into the courtyard.

Hands grabbed me, arms wrapping around my waist as a hard body pressed along the length of my back, buttocks, thighs. Fear knocked the breath out of me. Before I could find the breath to scream a voice said, low in my ear, "Cassidy."

I sagged against Joe. "Jesus, you scared the shit out of me."

"I'm sorry." He turned me around and wound his arms around me again, now tucked hard against me front to front. "You scared the shit out of me, too, when I found you gone."

It had been several hours since I'd left. "How'd you get here?"

"Taxi. It took fucking forever to get one at this time of night out here. I think he thought I was crazy."

I chuckled against him. "You are crazy."

"Don't ever leave like that, Cassidy. Dammit."

"I left you a note."

"I don't care. You still scared the shit out of me," he repeated.

I realized he was shaking, and a wave of guilt washed over

me. "I'm sorry. I just needed to… I don't know what I needed. I just wasn't ready to say good-bye to this place."

"I know. I know." He dropped light kisses over my forehead and cheeks and nose. "It's one of the things I love most about you, Cassidy. You care so much. It's so hard for you to let go."

If only he knew.

He kissed me then. What started as a touch as sweet as the ones on my face grew harder, more insistent. Normally somewhat tentative and questing, his tongue now claimed mine. His fingers dug into my upper arms as if he could assuage his own fear by grabbing hold of me.

A thrill washed through me, from my plundered mouth to the tips of my hiking boot–clad toes, and more important places in between. Hurrah!

Joe walked forward, backing me up until I was flat against a rough stone wall. He leaned into me, and I could feel him from chest to thigh against my body. And against my thigh pressed a very aroused cock.

I got giddy for a second, and only his hands holding me, and my own threading through his hair and pulling him in closer, kept me on my feet. Hell, my feet were almost leaving the ground; I was on tiptoes trying to match him kiss for kiss, insistent grind for insistent grind. My stabilizing core was my abdomen—my aching nipples, my pulsing clit.

"I love you," he muttered against the curve of my neck as he nipped with his teeth, soothed with his tongue. "I want you. I need you," he said as he repeated the action, throwing me off guard with tiny flashes of erotic pain.

This was not normal Joe. Whether he'd read my mind, whether it was the magic of Pencraig, or whether finding me gone in the middle of the night had snapped something in him, I didn't know. Maybe all three, maybe none of the above.

I simply did. Not. Care.

I pressed my head back, arching against him, opening my throat to him. The stars swam in the night sky in my unfocused gaze.

"We..." I tried, and lost my breath when he ducked his head and fastened onto my left nipple right through my T-shirt. The cotton soaked with his saliva, and when he pulled back for a moment, the air against the wet fabric felt icy cold against my heated, sensitive flesh.

"We..." I tried again, gulping for air. "We should...get back to the...B&B."

"No," he said, his voice sounding as strained as mine.

For a moment I couldn't even process what he'd said. He now had my right nipple in his mouth, his fingers working the other one, tweaking and pinching harder than he ever had, pushing me right to the edge of my limit. Or maybe my limit was greater than I thought. I thought I would very much like to find out.

Some part of my brain coughed up the reminder that I'd made a suggestion and he'd nixed it.

"No?" He didn't want to go back and have sex?

"No. Want you now. Here. Can't wait."

"But...someone might...might see." It took so much effort to form the thoughts. My cunt was throbbing, so sensitized that I could feel my swollen lips pressing against the seam of my jeans.

The fact was, Pencraig had a caretaker, a local man who came by at random times to make sure no hoodlum kids were holding a rave or, well, having sex in the great hall.

Not to mention that the land was bordered by other farms, and there was no telling who might wander by. Farmers. Neighbors. Hoodlum kids in search of a rave site.

"Don't care," Joe said. "It's dark. Nobody'll see."

Wow. I would've figured he'd care more than I did.

"What if they hear?"

"Guess you'll just have to keep quiet," Joe said.

For a moment I couldn't breathe. I wasn't actually a screamer (to be honest, Joe had never inspired me to those heights), but I was unthinkingly vocal. The idea that I'd have to deliberately silence myself flashed like an electrical impulse right down to my core. I heard my own whimper before I was even aware of making a sound.

Joe chuckled. "That's it, baby." He pulled the T-shirt over my head, tossed it somewhere. The stones were rough and cold against my back. I didn't care. My fingers were plucking at Joe's shirt, hauling it from his waistband, and he leaned away from me just long enough to peel it off.

I ran my fingers over his chest, the scattering of dark hair tickling my palms. His nipples were hard beneath my skimming touch.

Emboldened, needy, I reached down and pressed my hand against the hard, insistent length of him beneath his fly. He groaned, his hips flexing so he ground against my questing grasp.

My shower fantasy about the Tudor lord wasn't far off from this reality.

We had a brief moment of fumbling as I unlaced my damn hiking boots and stepped out of them (leaving my thick socks on to protect my tender soles from the gravel) so I could strip off my jeans. Joe's hand between my legs, his hoarse "Your panties are soaked" startled and thrilled me to the point that I almost pitched over.

Then he was on his knees in front of me, urging my stance wider so he could nuzzle the insides of my thighs. It was all I could do to keep from screaming—with impatience—as he took his own sweet time getting to my crotch.

When he finally pressed his mouth against my cunt, it wasn't with the careful solicitousness that he usually gave the task. It was with rapacious hunger, as if he hadn't eaten in days and I contained the sweetest nectar.

I stuffed my fist in my mouth to keep from screaming, because I really did want to when the orgasm slammed into me, wringing me until I was left limp and gasping.

Joe didn't leave me time to recover. He was on his feet, spinning me around so I faced the stone wall. I'd almost forgotten where we were and now I was reminded: in the open courtyard of a crumbling manor house, enacting our version of a passion that had flamed through generations back to the dawn of time.

Open to the night. Open to passersby. I no longer cared about that.

My cunt was still spasming from my first orgasm when Joe drove his cock into me. That definitely brought me up onto my toes.

We froze like that, with his cock buried in me, with me pulsing around him, the only sound that of our harsh breath. He buried his face in my shoulder and groaned something I couldn't decipher.

Then he curled his hands around my hips, and I had the presence of mind to grab the wall and hold on.

I bent over, arched my back so my ass thrust up, and met him lunge for lunge. His hips and belly slapped against my butt as we met again and again. The pressure was building for me again, from the feel of the hard length of him in me, from the urgent way he took me, from the vulnerable position I was in. From the open sky and looming ghostly walls and the possibility of eyes, live or ghostly, witnessing our frenzied union.

I was peaking, urging Joe on through hissed breath, when he

broke and came, his thrusts turning short and staccato and my name tumbling from his lips.

Afterward, it occurred to me that I didn't think he'd ever made a sound before when he'd come.

We had sleeping bags in the car, and camping pads, for those digs when we were too far from civilization to go for a real bed every night, and Joe got them from the car. We curled up together, propped against the wall, both of us loath to leave Pencraig just yet; saying good-bye in our own way.

Good-bye to the house, hello to each other.

We talked about everything and nothing. About our jobs, about preservation of historic sites, about our relationship, about sex, about how it was a good thing the pub was far enough away that the landlady wouldn't have wandered by because surely we would have given her a heart attack.

At some point we must have dozed off. I don't know what woke me, at the first light of dawn, but suddenly I was awake, alert. The sky was gray, the stars fading. A wren sang nearby.

And a small cluster of dark objects were darting overhead, dipping and wheeling almost faster than I could follow, before shooting into the black window of the north tower.

"Bats," I said aloud in wonder.

"What?" Joe stirred, blinked. Then he took my head in his hands and gave me a toe-curling kiss. "Morning."

"Morning." What had we been talking about? "Bats! I saw bats—they're roosting in the north tower."

"I had no idea you had a vampiric bent," Joe said.

I swatted at him. "Bats are protected in Wales," I said. "Remember that seminar we took? By law you can't disturb their roosting place."

"Oookay." Joe wasn't a fast waker. Hey, he'd had a rough night. I took sympathy on him.

"If Pencraig's a roost for bats, it can't be disturbed or damaged." A knot in my stomach, one I hadn't really been aware of until now, began to loosen. "It can't be developed in any way that would affect the bats."

They weren't, we learned after we sent in our report and a bat expert had been dispatched to examine the evidence, just any old bats. They were greater horseshoe bats, and only about a thousand were left in Wales. Fewer than ten lived at Pencraig, and could easily have been overlooked.

Take that, luxury resort developer!

We'd saved Pencraig.

Time would tell about the status of the rest of things. But the number one skill you learn as an archeologist is patience.

Except, of course, when it comes to sex. With that, impatience can be a virtue.

(S)PAN(K)CAKES

Kristina Wright

Know what I want for breakfast?"

Adam nuzzled my neck, still half asleep on a Sunday morning. "Mmm…sex?"

"Pancakes," I said.

"Then sex?"

I laughed at his eagerness and tousled his hair. "Maybe. C'mon. I'll make you pancakes and then we'll see."

We padded out to the kitchen, Adam in his boxer briefs and me in just a T-shirt and boyshorts. Adam swatted my ass when I bent to get out the mixing bowl from the cabinet.

"Hey!"

"Just trying to help," he said with a sleepy grin. "I'm getting hungry."

His leer told me he was hungry for more than pancakes.

"If you want to help, why don't you get the milk and butter out of the fridge?"

He gave me another smack. "I'd rather bend you over the counter—"

"Milk and butter!"

"Yes, ma'am." He saluted, rumple-haired and bare-chested, looking so delicious in the morning light streaming in the window.

I put the cast-iron skillet on the stove and added a quarter-sized dollop of oil. Then I assembled the dry ingredients in a glass bowl. Flour, sugar, baking powder, a little salt, some spices. Adam put the quart of milk and a stick of butter on the counter next to me and nuzzled my neck before swatting my ass again.

"I need an egg, too."

"You're a demanding wench."

"Hardly," I laughed, as I measured off three tablespoons of butter and put it in a coffee mug. I popped it in the microwave for thirty seconds. "I'm cooking for you, not the other way around. I am but your obedient serving wench."

"Obedient, huh?"

I ignored the suggestive tone in his voice as I took the melted butter out of the microwave. He got an egg from the refrigerator and handed it to me without a word. I could feel him standing behind me as I poured the milk into another bowl and added the egg and butter. I whisked the ingredients together slowly as I added a splash of vanilla, almost willing him to do what I knew he was going to do.

"You want it, don't you?" he whispered behind me.

I halted, midwhisk. "Hmm? What are you talking about?"

"You're practically sticking your ass out for it."

I stood up straight. "I am not."

"Yes, you are. You were waiting for me to spank you."

"Only because you've been smacking me since we got up," I argued, pouring the wet ingredients over the dry ingredients and returning to my whisking with increased vigor.

"So, you don't want it?"

"No." I didn't sound terribly convincing even to myself. "I'm trying to make pancakes."

Adam moved away to stand against the counter, arms crossed over his bare chest. His bare, sexy chest. "I see. And I'm distracting you?"

"Yes," I said, swallowing hard. "You are."

He shrugged. "Okay. I'll leave you alone."

"Oh. Okay." I looked at the pancake batter, well mixed and ready to be put on a hot pan.

Adam watched as I carried the bowl to the stove. I tried not to look at him. I was annoyed, but I wasn't going to tell him that. My ass was still tingling from that last slap and I wanted more. I wanted a lot more. He knew that and knew I was just playing coy, but he'd called my bluff and I was too rebellious to tell him what I wanted.

I scooped pancake batter from the bowl with a measuring cup and carefully poured it into the hot skillet. The batter sizzled, sending up that floury-sweet smell of pancakes that's so perfect on a Sunday morning.

"You're mad."

I ignored him, scooping and pouring more batter into the pan. When I had three pancakes cooking, I said, "I'm not mad. I just need the spatula. Would you get it for me?"

I heard him rummaging around in the gadget drawer behind me. "You want it?"

"Yes, I want it."

He smacked me with the spatula. "All you had to do was ask."

I yelped. "Hey! Knock it off. I'm cooking."

"Oh, sorry. I thought you wanted it."

I bit my lip. The last time I told him to stop he had...well... stopped. The pancakes were just beginning to bubble and would need to be flipped in a minute or two.

"I want it," I said, very deliberately. "I want it now."

Even though I was expecting it, the slap of the plastic spatula made me jump. He spanked each cheek once, hard enough that I whimpered.

"How was that?"

I kept my eyes on the pancakes. Another thirty seconds and they would definitely need to be flipped or they would burn.

"I said, I want it." I leaned over the stove, as if to get a closer look at my bubbling pancakes. "I really want it now."

"Your ass looks delicious," he said, giving it another slap with the spatula.

"I need to flip the pancakes now." I was a little breathless as I reached behind me for the spatula.

Adam handed it over and I quickly turned each of the pancakes. They were perfect, golden brown. "Mmm. They look good."

"Mmm, you look good," Adam said, applying his hand to my ass.

I whimpered at the warm slap of his hand, so different from the cold spatula. He smacked me again and I closed my eyes, breathing in the sweet scent of pancakes and reveling in the tingling heat spreading through my bottom.

"I think your pancakes are done," he said.

I opened my eyes and saw that he was right. The edges were perfectly brown. I sighed, completely disinterested in pancakes now, and slid the three pancakes off onto a plate.

"Why don't you let me hold that spatula while you pour the batter?" Adam asked, his voice telling me exactly what to expect.

I tried not to appear too eager as I handed over the spatula. Tried and failed. Adam spanked me with it before I had even scooped more batter. I yelped and jumped, leaving a trail of batter down the side of the mixing bowl.

"Messy girl," he growled, spanking me again.

My goal was to pour the batter as quickly as possible. I succeeded in pouring batter into three misshapen circles as the spanking continued. I whimpered with every slap, watching my sad little pancakes sizzle in the hot skillet. A trickle of perspiration—as much from leaning into the stove as from the heat radiating from my ass to my pussy—trickled between my breasts.

"Harder," I said breathlessly, hanging on to the edge of the stovetop and thrusting my ass out for it.

Adam obliged my demand, smacking me hard with the flat part of the spatula until I moaned. My eyes fluttered closed again as I gave myself over to the spanking. My pussy throbbed with every smack and heat spiraled through me. I ached to stroke my clit until I came.

"Pull your panties down."

I trembled as I obeyed. I was in a different world now, willing to do whatever Adam asked in order to get the satisfaction I needed. I tugged my panties down my thighs until they fell to the floor.

"Good," Adam said. "Now I can see what I'm doing to you."

"You like this, don't you?"

I felt him press against me, his erection hard against my hot ass. "What do you think?"

I moaned as I pressed against him, the fabric of his boxer briefs feeling rough against my tender flesh.

He stepped back and quickly administered a series of hard whacks with the spatula, stopping as suddenly as he started.

I whimpered, wanting more.

"Time to flip your pancakes, bad girl."

I fumbled to take the spatula from him, feeling clumsy and slow. I wasn't thinking about cooking anymore. I awkwardly flipped the pancakes while he rubbed my ass, taking away some of the sting. He knelt behind me and I felt him kiss each enflamed cheek.

"Mmm. You smell like pancakes," he murmured. The lick of his tongue between my cheeks made me shiver. "I wonder how you'd taste with maple syrup?"

"The pancakes are flipped." I handed him the spatula and bent over again.

Adam chuckled. "Anxious little wench, aren't you?"

I nodded, thrusting my bottom out for him. "Please?"

"Whatever you want, baby." He slapped me hard and I nearly screamed.

"I want to come," I murmured.

"Touch yourself."

It was all the encouragement I needed. With one hand gripping the stove, I pressed two fingers against my pussy and dragged my wetness up to my swollen clit. I stroked myself as Adam spanked me, each slap sending a tremor through me. I wouldn't last long. I was so hot with wanting, it would only take a moment or two until I was coming. I closed my eyes, absorbed in the feeling of my clit between my fingers, so wet and hard, and the stinging slaps on my ass that were sending me over the edge.

"Your pancakes are burning."

I nearly growled my frustration. Without a word, I took the spatula from Adam and slipped three more pancakes onto the plate. I handed him the spatula again, eagerly returning to my spanking pose and intent on getting off, but he had other ideas.

"I think there's enough batter for a couple more pancakes."

"Seriously?"

He whacked me, hard. "Don't be sarcastic. This was your idea."

I was cursing my clever idea as I poured the last two pancakes. "There. Happy?"

Another whack, as hard as the previous one. "Clearly, being spanked makes you more rebellious."

I slipped my hand down between my thighs again. "Do it. Spank me," I said urgently. "I'm so fucking hot."

He gave me what I wanted, spanking me hard and steady as I rubbed my clit. My bottom felt swollen and sensitive, and I whimpered from the sting that lingered after each smack.

"Your ass is getting so red," he murmured.

I could envision what he saw, my bottom thrust out for his pleasure, red from the spanking and shiny from the oil in the pan. I closed my eyes and moaned, grinding on my fingers as he spanked me.

"Fuck me."

I heard the clatter of the spatula on the floor, then Adam's cock bumping against my hand. I reached between my legs and guided him to my clit, stroking myself with the head of his cock before guiding him to my entrance. With one quick shove he was buried inside me, filling me up. I was so hot and wet for him, there was no need for him to go slow and take his time. The spanking he'd given me had been more than enough foreplay and now my body was begging for much-needed release.

He gripped my hip with one hand and my long hair with the other. I arched my back as he tugged at my hair, feeling the sharp tingle of pain at my scalp contrasting with the throb of warmth in my bottom. The sensations clashed in a tangle of pleasure as he pumped into me with hard, steady thrusts. I got off on the dual sensations of pain, strumming my clit in time with his cock going into me. Orgasm rushed over me in a powerful wave of heat and wetness that nearly buckled my knees. I held tight to the stove as Adam supported me with his hands and cock, thrusting hard into me.

My pussy squeezed the length of his cock, rippling with my

long, slow orgasm. As wet as I was, he had a snug fit as my body gripped him. He moaned, curling over my back as he pumped into me. I dragged my wet fingers over the length of him as he started to come, reveling in the heat and weight of his cock. I tightened my pussy around him, feeling the last vestiges of my waning orgasm. Then, with a final thrust and a bellowing groan, he went still against me. I could feel the pulse of his cock buried inside me as my pussy milked him of his orgasm and I clenched around him, eliciting another moan of pleasure.

Sweat slick and hot from both the spanking and my proximity to the stove, I opened my eyes to see two charred pancakes sending up curls of smoke. I started laughing, nearly collapsing under Adam's weight. He moaned, no doubt from the way my pussy undulated along his sensitive cock.

"I burned my pancakes," I gasped, as he slid from me. "And I'm pretty sure the others are cold."

He gave my tender ass a light swat. "I guess you'll just have to make another batch."

It didn't sound like such a bad idea.

(S)pan(k)cakes

Ingredients
1½ cups all-purpose flour
1½ tablespoons sugar
3½ teaspoons baking powder
¾ teaspoon salt
½ teaspoon cinnamon
¼ teaspoon nutmeg
1¼ cups milk
1 egg, lightly beaten
1 teaspoon vanilla extract

3 tablespoons butter, melted
1 tablespoon cooking oil, for frying pan

Directions

In a large bowl, sift together the flour, sugar, baking powder, salt, cinnamon and nutmeg. In a smaller bowl, combine the milk, egg, vanilla and melted butter. Pour the liquid ingredients over the dry ingredients and mix until nearly smooth. Set aside for 10 minutes.

Heat a lightly oiled frying pan over medium-high heat. Use a ¼ cup measuring scoop to pour the batter into the frying pan. Flip pancakes when small bubbles begin to form and brown lightly on both sides.

Serve warm, plain or with your favorite toppings.

Makes 6 large pancakes.

CLOTHES MAKE THE MAN

Emilie Paris

"Dress yourself up for me," Cameron said on Monday night. "You know what I like, Charlotte."

I did of course. After nearly a year together, I know exactly what turns on my man.

I have high-class tastes. That's the way I like to put it. My boyfriend says I bask in the lap of luxury. But when he says that, all thoughts of diamonds and expensive footwear disappear from my mind. Because even if I do like to doll myself up like some Parisian runway model, the lap Cameron's referring to is his own.

I looked at the clothes in my closet, the fur-trimmed cardigan, the red-sled Louboutins, and all I could see was me over Cameron's lap, my panty-clad ass in the air, my stockinged feet kicking.

"I'm waiting," Cameron said in a tone of voice that let me know he wouldn't wait for very much longer. He was sitting behind me on the edge of the bed. I could feel his eyes on me.

At the moment, I only had on a pair of scarlet knickers and a matching satin bra. If I wasn't careful, he'd start before I was ready. And satin doesn't offer much protection when a spanking's on the menu.

The clothes blurred in front of my eyes. I keep my closet in color-coded order, from midnight black on the left through all the rainbow colors, ending with pristine white on the right. But nothing called out to me. Nothing screamed *spanking*.

"Charlotte..." His tone was growing more menacing by the second.

Frantic, I stuck my hand into the closet and reached for the first thing my fingers landed on. I had to laugh as I pulled out the hanger. I'd chosen a navy blue suit, formfitting, but cut in a man's style. I turned around and held the outfit up in front of me. Cameron's lips curled in a half smile.

"Wasn't exactly what I was thinking."

"I know."

When he has spanking on the brain, he generally likes to see me in something more schoolgirl kicky: a little plaid skirt or a navy blue jumper, high-heeled Mary Janes and white kneesocks.

"But we could make that work," Cameron continued.

He left the room while I got dressed, giving me privacy. I worked as fast as I could. Nearly in a trance, I began to set the stage. I lit rows of candles on the windowsill and on the edge of the dresser. I dragged the heavy-backed chair to the center of the room, my fingers on the leather, my heart starting to pound. I wanted to be over Cameron's lap already, eager to be in the scene I was already so deeply entrenched in. But anticipation is an important part to our games. Absence doesn't necessarily make the heart grow fonder, but waiting definitely makes my pussy pulse.

Then I got dressed: crisp white shirt, the navy suit, a red tie, black oxford shoes. I caught a glimpse of myself in the mirror over our dresser, and then (at the very last minute, hearing Cameron's steps out in the hallway), I had an idea.

"Wait..." I called out.

His footsteps halted. I could imagine him standing right outside the door.

"I'll tell you when I'm ready."

I could imagine him standing there, interest piqued, cock hard. I went to my dresser and pulled out a toy, fixed the rest of the scene, then opened the door.

"Bad girl," he said softly, "making me wait."

"Bad boy," I responded, just as softly, watching as Cameron tilted his head at me. I saw confusion in his deep blue eyes, and I acted immediately. Before he could grab me, before he could say a word, I sat down in the leather chair. "Bend over, baby," I said, patting my thighs. "Time for your spanking."

"Charlotte..."

"Don't make me ask twice."

How many times had he spoken to me like that? How many ways had I found myself positioned for his firm hand, or his leather belt, or his paddle? Why had I never thought to respond in kind? What had the suit brought out in me?

Of course, Cameron didn't have to obey. He could have told me to get my ass out of the chair. He could have refused to take even one step forward. But he didn't. Instead, he walked toward me, then bent himself over my lap.

I grinned to myself. I couldn't believe the rush of power that flared through me. Without hesitation, I slapped my hand against his ass. I knew I hadn't hurt him. My palm met the resistance of his blue jeans, and I know from many past experiences that a hand spanking through denim doesn't do much harm. But I wanted to see how far he'd let me go.

I smacked him again, and then I said, "Stand up and take down those jeans."

When he stood, I saw the look in his eyes, a look I recognized from seeing the same expression in the mirror so many times before. He was loving this. He was needing it.

Cameron pulled down his jeans and bent back over my lap. He even raised his hips, begging with his body for me to continue.

I smacked my hand against his boxers, and I could feel how hard his cock was. I gave him five strokes like this before pulling the waistband of those striped boxers down to his thighs. Now, I took a moment to admire his naked ass. God, he had a beautiful body. I thought of how many times he'd admired my curves from the same position of power. Then I let my hand land on his bare skin. The rush of pleasure was amazing to me. My palm meeting his naked ass sent a electrifying jolt through my whole body. Why had we never done this before? Why had we never even tried?

I spanked him over and over, delighting in the handprint-shaped marks I was leaving on his previously pale skin. Cameron took the spanking like a pro. He didn't squirm. He didn't beg. He didn't make any sound at all. But I could feel his cock against my thigh, and I knew he was turned on. Maybe he was as surprised as I was by this new facet of our relationship. Maybe he was stunned into silence.

I wanted to help him make noise.

Deftly, I reached behind the chair and gripped the paddle that had been lying on the floor, the one I'd hidden right before he walked in the door. I didn't tell him to steel himself. I didn't warn him what was coming. I simply slapped that glossy weapon against his ass and waited for his response.

The tremor that ran through him was immediate and intense.

But he didn't tell me to stop and he didn't try to get up. That gave me all the information I needed. I spanked him again, and again. Each time I let the paddle land on his naked ass, I imagined what the pain was like for me when I was in a similar submissive position. My pussy grew wetter with every blow, and I could tell that Cameron was growing even harder. His cock was a solid pole against my leg.

"Such a bad boy," I murmured. "Getting all hard from a spanking. Clearly, it's been far too long since your last punishment."

Who knew I could talk like that, that there were words like those in my head, words that came easily to my tongue? I'd never even fantasized about a scenario like this one, and yet disciplining Cameron felt surprisingly natural.

I heated his ass good and proper for him, and when I was right on the verge of coming from the thrill alone, I pushed him off my lap. Cameron stared up at me, waiting. He looked like a puppy dog, his golden hair messy, his cheeks flushed. Sure, I understood what he wanted. I'd taken the front seat. He expected me to drive us to the finish line.

Quickly, I kicked off my shoes then unzipped my slacks and pulled them off along with my knickers. Then I positioned myself on the edge of the bed, my thighs spread wide.

"Eat me," I told him, and he crawled forward immediately, kicking off his jeans and boxers, so that he was now half naked, wearing only his white T-shirt. Pressing his face to the split of my body, he began to lick my clit in delicious, dreamy circles.

Oh, god that felt good. I leaned back on my arms and pushed my pussy right into his handsome face. I locked my legs around him, holding him as close to me as I possibly could. And then I let myself come, bucking hard against his lips and tongue, taking every last bit of pleasure from the ministrations of his mouth.

I couldn't remember ever coming so quickly, but spanking him had brought me right up to the brink.

When I was done, I looked down at Cameron. His lips were all glossy with my juices, and his eyes had that hungry glow in them. He wanted his own release. But I wasn't ready to let him get there yet.

"On the bed," I told him, as I slipped my slacks back on, naked now underneath them. Cameron looked horrified. I think he believed I was going to let him fuck me. But we weren't there yet. We weren't even close.

While he spread himself out on the bed, I pulled his leather belt out from the loops of his discarded jeans.

"Wrong way," I told him. He was faceup on the bed. I wanted him facedown.

Meekly, humbly, my sweet boy rolled over. I could just imagine how the mattress felt against a cock so hard.

"We'll start with ten," I said, and Cameron groaned. The noise twisted something deep inside of me. I was getting to like this new partnership. The new me.

With ease, I doubled up the leather and slapped the belt against Cameron's ass. His cheeks were already rosy from the paddle. Now, I wanted to see the welts bloom. Cameron kept himself entirely still, but that wasn't enough.

"I didn't think I'd have to say," I began, "that I expect you to count."

"One," he said.

"Good try. We're going to call the first one a practice blow."

I struck him again.

This time, when he said, "One," I said, "Now, ask me for another."

There was silence from the bed. He didn't want to ask. But from the way his hips were shifting on the mattress, I could tell he craved more pain.

"Ask me, Cameron, or I'll put a ball gag in your mouth, and then *I'll* determine exactly how many strokes you'll take. Let me warn you that what you think you can take and what I think you can take may be wildly differing numbers."

"May I please have another?" he murmured.

"Louder."

"May I please have another?"

I hit him again.

"Two," he said, and then, without being prompted this time, "May I please have another?"

"Mistress."

Silence.

"Ball gag," I threatened.

"May I please have another, Mistress?"

I hit him a third time. This was fun. I could do it all night. Together, we made our way up to ten, and then I saw Cameron's body relax. He thought we were done. He thought he'd made it to the end.

"Did I tell you to stop asking?"

"But..."

"Did I tell you to stop asking?"

"You said..."

God, he was slower than I'd thought.

"Did I tell you to stop asking?"

A deep sigh, then, "May I have another, Mistress?"

I hit him fiercely. He didn't hesitate to say, "Eleven. May I please have another, Mistress?"

We went to twenty, so that his ass was crisscrossed with plum-colored lines from the belt. I don't think I'd ever seen something so beautiful before. I'd created those lines. I'd done this to him. I'd give him something he needed.

I made sure the last stroke hurt. He cried out, for the first time, and then I knew he was done.

"Roll over."

Grateful, with tears in his eyes, Cameron rolled over on the bed. His cock was hard, and my pussy was so wet.

Quickly, I stripped off my clothes once more—all of them—the suit jacket, white shirt, slacks. I was me once more when I climbed onto the bed, and Cameron seemed to know that. He gripped my hips and pulled me down onto him, and then he let me ride him. I fucked him as hard as I could, swiveling my body, getting his cock so deep inside of me, then pushing up with my thighs before sliding down once more.

At least, I was almost me. A remnant of the Mistress side of me remained.

"Next time," I said, "I'm going to get a strap-on. Next time, I'm going to be the one who fucks you."

"Oh, Jesus."

"You'd like that, wouldn't you, Cam? You'd like me to split apart your asscheeks, pour on some lube, and fuck the shit out of you."

"God, yes."

Cameron didn't seem to even feel the pain from his recent whipping. He drove up inside me with such fierce force, and when he came, I came with him, reaching down to touch my clit as the shivering pleasure flickered through us both.

Afterward, Cameron pulled out of me, and then held me in his arms. He seemed to want to know that I was his girlfriend once more—that I'd shed my skin, that we were equals, partners. He stroked my hair from my face, kissed my lips, kissed my palms, and my wrists.

"How'd you know?" he asked softly.

"I didn't."

"Then what made you do that?"

"I don't know."

His mouth to my ear, his voice a whisper, he asked, "Will you do that again?"

"Whenever you need," I told him. "Whenever you want."

"But how will you know?"

I smiled at him, and looked down at the crumpled suit on the floor. "You just leave my suit on the bed," I said. "I'll do the rest. Because you know what they say? Clothes make the man...."

PLAYING ROUGH

Kat Black

Click, clack, click…

The woman's heels spike the concrete floor, staccato beat rebounding off the hard, straight lines of the subterranean tunnel. Each step echoes, a solitary sound in an otherwise oppressive silence. Overhead, badly spaced strip-lighting runs the length of the walkway, casting intermittent pools of brightness among dark, dingy shadows.

The hour is late, yet the woman's appearance remains as immaculate as when she'd arrived shortly after dawn. Makeup flawless, hair shiny and sleek, tidy in a French twist; tailored jacket and pencil skirt virtually crease free despite hours of corporate grind. Her look is polished and professional, conservative but for the stacked, black patent ankle boots adding a hint of fetish and six inches to her diminutive stature.

Briefcase in hand, the woman heads toward the far end of the tunnel, to the door marked STAFF CAR PARK. On the other side her sports car awaits, compact and shiny, the only vehicle to be found in the executive parking bays at this time of a Friday night.

Thud.

At the top of the stairwell behind her, the walkway's only other access door closes heavily. The woman starts, surprise flashing across her composed features, the expression transforming into a questioning frown. Pausing, she turns to watch the stairwell with alert, uneasy eyes.

Nothing happens. Nobody appears.

Frown deepening, pulse point ticking in the curve of her neck, the woman starts on her way again, taking no more than a handful of steps before a whisper of something halts her in her tracks. She scans her seemingly deserted surroundings with a wide, searching gaze.

"Hello?" she calls, the single word repeating, hollowing, then fading back into thick silence.

Again, she waits. Again, nothing. No noise but the low hum of the strip-light overhead.

Perhaps it's the static electricity trapped in the stale, stagnant air that causes the woman's skin to prickle, the hairs all over her body to rise. Perhaps it's something more primal, basic instinct, impelling her to go. Get out. Now.

Click, clickety, clickclack...

The woman's steps falter as she hastens away, passing through a patch of light, into shade, then light again. That's when she hears it.

Tap. Tap. Tap. Tap.

Footsteps. Steady, distinct. Heading her way.

Without slowing, the woman throws a look over her shoulder, squinting against the brightness overhead. There! In the shadows of an unlit area some way back, a blacker shade of darkness moves. Someone is there. Someone large in form, menacingly male.

Panic stamps her features.

Clickclackclickclackclick...

Breaking into a run, the woman flees toward the exit, speed severely hampered by skirt and heels.

Instantly, the chase is on. Footfalls pound after her in long-gaited strides, gaining easily, quickly. The skin between her shoulder blades draws tight, tiny hairs ripple at her nape.

Then hard hands are on her, jerking her off her feet, hauling her back against a big, powerful body. A large palm clamps over her mouth, cuts short her scream.

A minute of frantic conflict—tousling shuffles, grunting scuffles—ends with her crushed between hard muscle and solid wall, jacket pulled roughly down to her elbows, pinning her arms to her sides, briefcase and bag on the floor.

An unyielding length presses against her from behind, envelops her from top to toe, imprisons her.

"Scared?" a deep male voice taunts in her ear. "You should be, given the things I'm about to do to you."

Trapped, chest heaving, eyes wild, the woman snaps her teeth at the fingers held over her mouth, only to have them shift out of harm's way, tighten around her jaw like a vise.

"Bite me and you'll regret it." The voice grates. "Scream, and I promise you it'll be even worse."

Threats issued, the man's hand drops from her mouth, joins the other busy hitching her skirt up over her thighs. "I'll give you one warning. Don't fight me. I'm bigger, much stronger. You'll only lose."

"Please...please," the woman stutters. "What do you want?"

"I'd have thought that'd be obvious to a smart woman like you." Skirt out of his way, the man inserts a leg between hers, uses his shoe to prize both her feet apart. "Spread your legs. Wide."

"Please. I...I have money. In my purse," she offers, twisting her neck to face him.

"Don't turn around." The man shoves forward, broad chest restricting her movements, knocking the air from her lungs. Lower down, the fabric of his trousers scrapes and the metal teeth of his zipper dig into her newly exposed skin. Between their bodies his erection presses, hard and huge, every inch rigidly defined. "You know damn well it's not your money I'm after."

Stepping back a pace, the man splays one hand over the woman's shoulder blades, keeping her pushed to the wall while the other smooths over the pale cheeks of her buttocks.

"Very nice. Black thong and hold-ups. Did you put these on especially for me?" With a couple of one-handed yanks the skimpy underwear is down around the woman's knees, the thin straps stretched taut.

"Don't..." She rears back against the man's hold.

Suddenly he's covering her again, plastering his body over her smaller frame, dominating her. "Don't what?" he demands. "Do this?" The fingers of one hand plunge into her cleft from behind, parting folds, invading soft, secret flesh, making her gasp in shock.

"Or this?" The man's other hand twists in the woman's hair, ruining the careful style with a few quick tugs. Pins scatter, pinging on the floor. Fisting the loosened strands, he arches her head back onto his shoulder, lowers his mouth to her ear.

"Haven't you realized yet? You don't get to have a say in this. You're mine. To do with as I please..." Between the woman's legs, his fingers circle her entrance, two drive inside her, jolting a groan from her throat, proving his words.

"And it pleases me to start by mussing up all this precious perfection." Withdrawing his fingers, the man brings them to the woman's lips, smears gloss and musk together, pushes them deep into her mouth. "It might impress the starched suits you work with, but it doesn't fool me for a minute. I've been watching you, you see. Watching and waiting for an opportunity to get you all alone, to get my hands on you so I can put a crack in that ice-cool façade of yours."

Fitting one restraining thigh snugly between the woman's, the man eases a fraction back from the wall; his fingers slip from her mouth, draw a wet trail from chin to chest. "And now that I've finally got hold of you, I'm going to take you apart, baby. Bit by bit. Going to make you burn." Sliding under the scooped neckline of her fitted top, his hand burrows into her lacy bra, squeezes one hard-tipped breast.

"Good girl. I've barely got started and already you're excited. Or are you just feeling the cold?" Using his grip on the woman's hair to angle her face toward him, the man pinches the distended nipple tight between finger and thumb, sweeps his tongue over her lips as they part for an involuntary gasp. A deep, masculine rumble of approval issues from him.

"Hell. Tastes like sticky sweet excitement to me." The man's hands shift, tug the woman's top and bra high up onto her chest, capture the weight of her breasts as they spill free. "You ready to take some more?" He plucks and rolls both nipples, bucks and rolls his hips.

The woman's body flinches and squirms under the assault. She shudders as the reflex action causes her spread sex to grind against the muscled thigh between her legs. The man immediately adjusts his stance, rocking her core harder against him.

"Oh, yeah. So sensitive, so fiery. You're ready to take whatever I want to give you."

A half whimper escapes the woman as she shakes her head. "No," she denies. "I...I can't."

"Oh, but you can..." The man drags her back a couple of steps.

"And you will..." He tears the jacket from her arms, discards it.

"Right now." His hands bend her forward at the waist.

"Put your palms flat on the wall in front of you. Arms straight. Feet wide apart," he orders.

Balance suddenly precarious, the woman obeys, steadying herself as he grabs her hips, raises her arse, positions her as he will. Without preliminary, the man drops to a crouch behind her, his thumbs spread her slit wide. "Very pretty." So close, the rush of his hot breath tickles her most private places as he speaks. "All pink and pouty and open for me. Good enough to eat."

The woman's muscles spasm at the first touch of his tongue. "Don't move." He grips her thighs, holds her immobile as he runs the warm, wet tip firmly from clit to crack, growling.

"You taste like sex already. All wet and juicy, your cunt welcoming me to slide right in." Penetrating her with his tongue, the man skims the woman's inner walls with a swirling lick. Moaning, she locks elbows and knees tight. Shivers chase over her skin as she drops her head forward, sucks in a shaky breath.

The man straightens and makes short work of loosening his fly fastenings, lowering trousers and boxers together. Taking his cock in one hand, he rubs the engorged head up and down between the woman's damp folds before guiding it to her entrance. His other hand grasps a handful of her hair, pulls her head back, bows her spine.

"Brace yourself, baby. I'm going to fuck you now. So hard, so fast and deep, you'll never forget it."

With that the man's hips surge forward, driving his iron-hard erection into her. His forceful grunt mingles with her startled shout; then he thrusts once, twice more, stuffing himself in to the hilt.

"Christ!" he chokes out, head thrown back, every muscle in his body snapped taut. "So tight, so fucking hot."

"No," the woman pants, trembling while the man's grip on her hair holds her impaled. "No... Too much."

"Not yet it isn't. Not until you've taken everything I've got." He withdraws halfway, forges forward again until his balls nestle tight against the lips of her sex.

The woman's cry sends echoes up and down the tunnel, her legs begin to fold beneath her. Encircling her with both his arms, the man holds her up, chest blanketing her spine.

"That's better," he says, voice squeezed rough. "Buried nice and deep so you can feel all of me." He begins to pump, fast, short jerks that keep him jammed tight up against her. His hands find the swinging weight of her breasts, fingers resume their torturous assault on the budded tips.

Under the ruthless barrage, the woman's body jars and jumps uncontrollably. Her whimpering pleas become a chant.

"Hearing you beg so sweetly really turns me on, baby, but you'rc asking me for the wrong thing." The man keeps up the punishing onslaught until her words are reduced to incoherent sobs of pleasure-pain and her nipples turn diamond hard to his touch. "See? Your lush little body is telling me that stopping is the very last thing you want me to do."

Large hands slide to the woman's waist as the man stands upright. Easing back a bit to gain more leverage, he changes his rhythm, uses long, powerful thrusts. In, out. In, out. Each sawing stroke is a relentless full-length glide from head to hilt; each hard hit home jolts a raw groan from the woman's throat.

"Christ, you're killing me," the man gasps, eyes focused on the point where their two bodies join. "You look so beautiful, taking my big cock all the way inside you." His hands curve around to the woman's arse, heels of his palms spreading her cheeks wide, opening her to his intent gaze. "So sexy down here—stretched to your limits around me, coating me in your juices. Fuck, just the sight of it makes me want to come."

The man's breathing becomes ragged, his measured thrusts grow erratic. "I'm losing it, baby. Going over the edge..." He reaches one hand around to spear into the thatch of wet curls between the woman's legs, scissoring the hardened bud of her clitoris between two fingers. "Taking you with me."

The woman's body bucks and writhes against him, her high-pitched keening fills the air. "Let go," he grinds out between bared teeth. "Come all over my cock." He punctuates the command with a push of his other thumb against the puckered rim of her anus. "Do it now."

"Oh, god!" the woman cries. "I'm com... I... Oh!" Knees buckling she screams, convulsing through her orgasm.

The man takes her weight to support her. Tendons strain, hips piston. "Christ, that's good. Like a fist... Ahh... Can. Barely. Move... Gonna come. Hard."

And he does, roaring his release, riding it out buried deep in the woman's shuddering body.

Moaning, drawing in great gasps of air, the man clasps the woman tight to him. Cock still embedded he shuffles and stumbles until his back hits the wall.

"God, Kat, please tell me I didn't hurt you." He all but collapses, cradling her to his chest, face pressed into the hair behind her ear. "You okay?"

"Mm, bloody wonderful," she replies, her body going limp, her tone dreamy. "How about you?"

He puffs out a mighty breath and leans his head back against the wall, eyes closed, a smile curling his lips. "Half dead and a happy man. That was fucking amazing."

"Literally," she chuckles. "Happy anniversary, husband."

"The first of many." He squeezes her. "I love you."

SEARCHING FOR HER

Kay Jaybee

Fifteen years ago I read my very first erotic story. From that moment I had a powerful recurring fantasy based entirely on its contents. Each relationship I've enjoyed since has had that one sexual expectation wrapped up in it.

Despite my efforts, I continually failed to find anyone with whom I could make my wildest dream come true. Then I met Mark. Once I'd shared my fantasy with him, he quickly became equally obsessed by it. So much so that he made the realization of it a mission for me, a quest that has led to many deliciously dirty encounters.

I investigated every club, dance floor, bar and meeting site possible searching for a woman who could turn our dreams to reality. The fact I eventually found her by accident, sitting at an ordinary table, in an ordinary café, sipping a ridiculously strong Americano, was my first surprise, the first of many.

Her disguise is perfect. She appears to be like every other thirtysomething female: average height, blue jeans, white shirt, black boots and long brown hair. The only clue to her true self is her incredible smile. It is literally dangerous and can alter her dark gray eyes from flirty, to sexy, to downright demonic in an instant.

It was those eyes that made me want to talk to her, for as soon as I spotted them staring at me, the hairs on the back of my neck began to tingle. The overcrowded nature of the café made it easy for me to ask for a seat at her table, but I was amazed at how readily she introduced herself.

I'm not sure why it felt okay to talk to Jo so candidly. It was almost as if her presence had been contrived somehow, for within a remarkably short amount of time we'd moved on from small talk, and it seemed natural for me to tell her about the search that I'd been sent on.

Jo's face glowed with mischief as she asked me for details of the encounters my pursuit had led me to so far. My gaze darted around the coffeehouse. This was not the sort of conversation that should be overheard, but something about Jo made me want to tell her everything. Luckily, the London fashion of each person being intent only upon him or her self was in evidence, and I felt safe enough to launch into my tale, albeit in hushed tones.

"Mark's requirements are, on the surface, simple. It doesn't matter how tall she is, where she's from, what color her skin, hair, or eyes are, as long as I find a woman he would like, who's willing to become part of a threesome, and who will do exactly as he says.

"I found the first woman that came close to his specifications in an S/M club. She was of similar height to my own, and her curling blonde hair contrasted nicely with my short black bob. The fact she was a client at that sort of club, and that her face was permanently lowered to the floor, proved she'd fulfill the 'doing what she was told' part of the deal.

"She wore only a maroon basque and stockings, no shoes, no collar of ownership, no jewelry, and as befitting her submissive poise, she carried no whip or paddle. Her blue eyes raised a fraction as I approached her, my heart thudding in my ears. She was gorgeously voluptuous, and I couldn't help but hope she'd be the one.

"The club itself was split into a series of rooms: general meeting places and dance floors, private rooms that were hired out by the hour; a men-only room, and a women-only room. It was into this final room that I asked her to accompany me. She smiled and nodded, but said nothing.

"Dimly lit, the room had rows of cream sofas against its walls, divided from each other with a modicum of discretion, by flimsy muslin curtains. I took her hand, surprised at how cold it was despite the heat of the club, and steered her to a free sofa. The second I asked her to sit down she obeyed. The woman, whose name I never did learn, was already waiting on my every command.

"Sitting astride her lap, our stocking tops rubbing together, I tilted her chin up so I could peer into her eyes. She stared back at my face, and I kissed her.

"The moment our lips met she came to life, giving as enthusiastically as she received. Grasping the laces that fastened the top of her basque, I yanked them loose, spilling her chest free. I held each heavy globe in my palms, squeezing and kneading until I was rewarded by a gentle nuzzling purr.

"Her nipples pushed against my hands. I bent my mouth to them, alternately licking and biting, until my blonde companion began to squirm beneath my weight. I didn't want her to come yet, and so I released her breast. Sliding to my knees, I rolled each of her stockings down her legs.

"As I worked, I glanced at her face and saw desire mingled with confusion. This was not how things usually went for her. She'd not received a single order since my initial request for her to sit, and her arms hung limply at her sides, uncertain. I continued, and with the stockings gone, began to caress each shapely pale calf in turn.

"My tits were beginning to feel tight within my satin bra, and I paused to unhook its clasp, watching with satisfaction as my temporary lover sighed longingly at their appearance. In need of some stimulation myself, I granted her permission to touch me. Soon my tits were being treated to an expert range of soft strokes, heavy nips with dazzling teeth, and teasing fingertips. Swiftly I found myself on the edge of orgasm, and robbed of the willpower to command her to stop.

"After that, my plans to make love to her gently, to discover as much about her talents as possible, were forgotten. We were merely a heady mixture of arms, legs, breasts, and illicit imaginings. She tasted of peaches, and I could have eaten from her all night, but I had a mission to complete. Once we had stilled, I held her close, and explained about my quest. I told her how I thought she'd be perfect for Mark and me. She listened quietly, then turned to me, and uttered the longest sentence of our evening together: 'I don't do men.'

"I couldn't believe it. I'm usually so attuned to that sort of thing. I guess I'd been blown away by my attraction to her. Mark would be disappointed, and I knew I would suffer a few strokes of his belt for my failure, but in truth, I never mind that."

I paused. Jo's eyes had blazed whilst I spoke, but now they simmered with amusement at my mistake. "She sounded lovely."

"She was, but not for Mark, and so I carried on looking."

"Tell me."

* * *

"The next time I came close was with a girl called Liz I'd encountered via a 'Threesomes Fun' website. I exchanged many emails with her before arranging to meet properly. Wisely, Liz wanted to know pretty much everything about Mark and..."

Jo broke through my story, "What is he like anyway? What does he look like?"

I smiled at her eager interest, "Mark is totally gorgeous. He's thirty-eight years old, about five feet eight, with short, brown, gray-flecked hair. His eyes are a deep dark hazel, and somehow incredibly honest, with lashes that would be the envy of anyone. They seem to make him appear at once vulnerable and powerful."

"I'm intrigued." Jo lifted the corner of her mouth into another devastating grin. "So, what happened with Liz?"

"I emailed her, describing Mark and myself. I told her I was bi, but that Mark was straight with a massive lesbian fantasy fixation, which I alone couldn't fulfill, but, was more than happy to make a reality for him.

"In return, Liz told me she was a petite five feet, with long ginger hair and green eyes. She was also bisexual, and enjoyed submission.

"I had high hopes when she agreed to meet for a drink, and was not disappointed when I first caught sight of her perched on a bar stool sipping a glass of wine.

"Watching her for a while before I approached, I wondered how long it would be before I managed to get her out of her black trousers and the fitting green top, which clearly revealed she wore no bra beneath. Her hair was..."

Jo reached out and placed a firm hand over my wrist, sending an unexpected shock wave of passion down my body. "Forget all that meeting and greeting bit. What was she like to fuck?

You did fuck her, didn't you?"

"I accompanied Liz to her small cluttered flat, but I was already having nagging doubts about her suitability. She had an unexpectedly whiny accent that I knew would drive Mark mad. But Liz was very attractive, and I was well up for sex. Anyway, successful or not, Mark would want a full report of my afternoon's research.

"We hadn't been through the door for more than a few seconds when Liz was pulling at my jacket, and my purple T-shirt was being yanked over my head. I don't think anyone has ever undressed me with such speed. Then she stepped back and appraised me. I could feel her piercing eyes devouring every inch of my flesh as I goose-pimpled with cold.

"Clicking on her stereo, Liz began to sway in time to the music, and then began to strip. It was obviously not the first time she'd done it, and I couldn't help but be impressed as she moved sensuously to the music, her cute plaits swinging provocatively as she eased off each garment.

"The slow beat of the music increased as the tracks changed, and Liz virtually ripped off her knickers to the faster tempo. My blood hammered in my veins as we stood, only a meter away from each other, totally naked, savoring the buildup of tension before we acted.

"I'd had certain ideas of how to play this encounter prior to my arrival, but now decided to go with the flow, to see what Liz would do.

"'On your knees.' The order sounded strange coming from such a squeaky voice, but the commanding glint in Liz's eyes was unmistakable, and so I obeyed.

"Seconds later I was on all fours, and a palm was slapping my arse with sharp regularity. I cried out under her smacks as Liz built up a rhythm, turning my buttocks from warm to roasting.

"As I swayed against her attack, a single probing digit began to push against my anus. Gently at first, its intrusive presence grew, and soon Liz was fingering me like a professional.

"Sweat dotted my back as she introduced a second finger, and then a third. My hole puckered and suckled at her digits, making her laugh in delight at how up I was for an arse fuck. Slipping her free hand between my legs, Liz teased my clit, doubling the knots in my stomach as she began to slap my pussy in time to the thrust of her fingers, and I found myself quivering and rocking against her.

"As my climax died away, Liz instructed me to stay exactly where I was. My arms ached, and I longed to collapse onto the floor, but Mark had trained me well over the last few months, and I remained where I was.

"I heard the click of a belt, and recognized it as a strap-on harness even before Liz had wordlessly lined the dildo's head up against my butt. Without ceremony, she slammed into me, making the walls of my back passage stretch farther, as the fake cock filled me to the hilt.

"Liz was breathing heavily, her chest and pigtails brushing my skin as she leant against my back. Then flicking the switch of a previously hidden remote, she made the dildo shoot into life. Massive vibrations ripped through us, tipping me into another orgasm and electrifying Liz's pussy, until her shrill yelps echoed in my ears.

"I did collapse then, trapped between her lightweight frame and the thinly carpeted floor."

"How did she take not being chosen?" Jo asked.

"She was disappointed, but Mark would have hated her voice, and to be honest, it got on my nerves a bit too. Also, despite her claims to the contrary, she was too openly dominant. Anyone who joins Mark has to keep that side of herself firmly under control, and I don't think Liz could have managed that. Shame really, she was pretty, and we had a brilliant fuck."

"You don't regret the encounter then?" Jo's smile became ever more suggestive.

"Not at all." I looked at my new companion, trying to gauge her reaction to everything I'd said. "Who could possibly regret an excellent piece of arse work?"

"Well I couldn't, that's for sure!" Jo laughed as she increased the pressure on my wrist. "May I ask some questions?"

"Of course." Without thinking what I was doing, I flipped my hand around so she could hold it properly, and experienced a second arousing twitch between my legs.

"What exactly does Mark want to do with the girl you find for him?"

"I honestly don't know. All he's told me is that once my search is completed I'll find out; until then I'm as much in the dark as the person I'm hunting for, apart from the part of the dream that was originally mine of course."

"I see. I guess you aren't going to tell me what that is?"

"Correct."

Jo nodded conspiratorially, "So, what sort of sex is Mark into?"

"Dirty, rough, dominant bondage."

"Interesting." Again, one corner of Jo's mouth rose in an evil beam. "I can't wait to meet him."

I didn't respond for a moment. My throat had gone very dry at the thought of having this woman holding me, kissing me, screwing me. Just the touch of her was making my knickers wet. "You want to meet him?"

"Yes."

"You think you could be the third person?" I couldn't keep the hope out of my voice.

"Don't you?" Her voice was steady and calm, and her eyes twinkled as they gazed into mine. I simply nodded. No other reply was necessary. I didn't even, as Mark would say, "need to test-drive her" to make sure he'd like her. I just knew he would.

I picked up my mobile and sent Mark a text: *I've found her.*

Seconds later he replied, *Bring her to me at 7pm tonight.*

I hadn't heard anything else from my lover before I arrived outside his home a little before seven. The palms of my hands were damp with perspiration, and I wiped them against the back of the short denim skirt Mark likes me to wear, which only just covers my black stocking tops.

Before I see Mark, I always feel slightly unsettled. He is such a controlling force in my life; my heart rate seems to double at just the sight of his glass front door. As I waited for Jo my apprehension grew. What if I'd got it wrong, and Mark didn't like her?

A few minutes later Jo emerged from a taxi, her slim legs also clad in stockings, and a short flared black skirt covering her tight arse. Her chest peeked suggestively out from a low-cut white blouse, and she wore knee-length black boots. Jo glowed with excitement, and suddenly I wondered why I'd been so concerned.

"Shall we?" I pointed to the hallway that led into the block of flats.

"Let's." Jo grasped my hand, and I experienced the same surge of warmth and hunger as I had in the café.

Mark's face was a picture as he opened the door, and I could tell that, on first impressions at least, Jo had met his criteria.

I studied Jo closely as she examined my partner. Desire flushed her face as Mark led us into his bedroom, and I heard her gasp as she saw the incongruous four-poster that dominated the space.

Mark sat in a leather chair he'd purposefully placed opposite the end of the bed. I could see the outline of his dick cramped against his jeans, and knew from the heaving of his chest that he was struggling to keep control of himself, now he was finally in the situation he'd dreamt of for so long.

Pointing to me he said, "Take her blouse off."

I trembled as I opened Jo's shirt, revealing a very sexy black bra which complemented her lightly tanned complexion perfectly.

"Now her skirt."

Again I obeyed.

"And her knickers, but leave her boots and stockings on."

I was temporarily surprised at how cliché his requests were, but as I stepped back and stared at her, I realized it was exactly how it should be. Jo looked incredible.

I'd guessed what was going to be asked of me next, and was already halfway to complying as Mark gestured to the bag of restraints he kept by the bed. "Her wrists."

Jo obligingly stretched her arms out for me to tie to the bedposts, allowing herself to be secured and made vulnerable.

"Gag her."

I fished around in the bag and produced two gags, one ball and one metal clamp. I brandished them in front of Mark questioningly.

"The ball."

I was relieved on Jo's behalf that he'd chosen the marginally more comfortable restraint, and applied the sphere between Jo's teeth, fastening the strap so it trapped her hair beneath its strong elastic.

"Take off her bra and suck her tits."

I didn't need to be told twice. Her breasts were as beautiful as I'd imagined, creamily smooth, with large nut brown areolas that felt pleasingly rough beneath my tongue.

I glanced up at Jo's face as I worked across her with increasingly hard kisses. She was staring at Mark, her eyes darting with want, her teeth clamping down against the gag to deflect the sensations I was creating, which the involuntary twitches in her legs told me were growing fast.

As I sucked, I began to wish Mark would make me take my top off, for my breasts were swelling and my nipples felt taut and constrained. No such instruction was forthcoming however, and I carried on with my task, painfully aware of my own arousal, as Jo's legs trembled, and her feet fidgeted against the plushly carpeted floor.

Mark's gruff voice bounced off the walls: "Stop what you're doing and tie her legs; she can't be trusted to keep still."

I reluctantly pulled away, noting the flash of loss that crossed Jo's face, before I widened her legs and attached her ankles to the bed frame with short buckled straps.

My lover's hand began to caress his cock as he observed the stranger before him, spread-eagled and completely within our power.

"Eat her."

I knelt, sweeping my tongue over her erect clit, feeling the vibrations of a muffled sigh as Jo bit into the rubber mask. Increasing my speed, I enjoyed the ripples of her approaching climax as they ran across her stomach.

"No one is to come." Mark's voice was harsh and tight, and I knew he was commanding his own body as much as ours.

I slowed my pace, circling my tongue around her pussy, rather than over her nub. Small specks of dribble were gathering at the corner of her lips. I longed to lick them away, to take off the gag and hear the noises she was making, but that was not my decision to make.

"Leave her."

It was a wrench to move away from the wonderful taste and aroma of Jo's sticky sex, but I did as I was told, and went to Mark's side.

Despite the tears of frustration that dotted at their corners, Jo's bright eyes shone, and I could see how much she was enjoying herself.

Mark hoisted me onto his lap and ripped my shirt open, dragging my tits over the top of my bra. He yanked at my right nipple, making me yelp as he stretched it as far as it would go, before mercifully letting go and attacking my left side.

His dick rubbed against my skirt's waistband, and I longed to hold it in my hand or take it into my mouth. Instead, he told me to stand and strip, which I did, very quickly.

I stole a glance at Jo as I stood naked, and was relieved to see lustful approval in her expression. Mark turned me to face him, knelt me down, and shoved his thick shaft into my mouth.

I relished Mark's salty sweet taste as I rolled him around my tongue, fully aware of the effect our show would be having on Jo, helpless and desperate for more stimulation. Mark removed his navy polo shirt, and I trailed my hands over his torso, making him moan softly.

He gently eased me away then, twisting me so that I was sideways to Jo, then he took off his trousers and boxers and, stunningly naked, slipped on a condom, before lifting me in his arms. I wrapped my legs around his waist as he pushed his cock into me.

I held on to Mark's neck, plastering his face with savage kisses, while he observed Jo watching us. Her eyes reflected frustration, but she didn't turn them away from the spectacle we were creating for her, and I couldn't help but be impressed by her self-control. I wondered if I'd have been tugging at my bonds by now if the roles had been reversed.

As Mark continued to plunge into me, I could feel my stomach fill with the first flutters of climax and was amazed when he let me come around his cock, and more amazed still when he cradled me lovingly as I came down from my temporary high.

He carried me to his chair, sat me down, and wiped stray hairs from my forehead. Once I'd caught my breath he said, "Undo her gag now. Kiss her better. Have a little fun, baby."

I moved fast, stunned by Mark's unprecedented sharing. Undoing the strap that held the ball gag, I gave Jo a second to maneuver her stiff jaw before launching onto her with a battery of greedy kisses, which she returned with a desperate joyful fervor.

Before she could find her voice, I slid a hand between her thighs and captured her groin. Encouraged by the gasp she uttered into my mouth, I cupped a breast with my other hand, tightening my fingers around her nipple. Distracted from my kisses, Jo's mouth fell open, and she began to pant with pleasure.

Mark came closer to us, his face flushed red, his skin darkening into blotches beneath his light chest hairs. "I think it's high time you lived out your teenage fantasy, don't you?"

My body, still high from the climax he'd unexpectedly allowed me to have, rushed with heady anticipation, as the image from the book I'd read so long ago entered my head.

Untying Jo, Mark led her from the bed to the middle of the floor. Grabbing a handful of her hair, he ordered her to her knees and elbows. Then he nodded to me, and I positioned myself above Jo. Straddling my legs over her thighs, I rested on my hands and knees over her luscious body, so that our pussies were lined up next to each other.

"Hell, you girls are just so beautiful!" Mark murmured as he towered over us. "You are such bad girls, my naughty bad girls." He carried on muttering his appreciation, till at last he rammed his dick between my legs, filling me for a blissful second before pulling out, leaving me woefully, deliciously empty, while he dived into Jo's waiting cunt.

I'm not sure which of us was groaning and mewling the loudest as Mark's sharp thrusts built in tempo, as he alternated between our bodies at a staggering pace. Balancing my weight carefully, I placed a hand beneath Jo's body and found her clit. Immediately, I was rewarded with a low moan of longing as I stroked it with the tip of one finger. Jo began to yelp and quake, her arms shaking with the effort of supporting our combined weight. Mark lunged into me for the final time, his cock pumping out spunk in a hot wave of ultimate satisfaction.

The second he was done, Mark pushed Jo and me to the floor. Rolling us over, he placed his large hands between our legs, kneading and stroking until we both spasmed again in mutual, overwhelming, mind-blowing pleasure.

Waking the next morning, tangled in the four-poster's crisp white sheets, I was momentarily puzzled to find three hands across my naked body, until I remembered I'd crashed into bed last night with the two sexiest people I'd ever met. Fresh desire flooded through me as I reflected on the evening before, and the final wonderful fulfillment of my doubled-up threesome fantasy.

I reached out my hands and began to circle stealthy fingers over their sleeping chests, one smooth and silky, the other downed with fine curling hairs....

A WEEK AND A WHIP

Allison Wonderland

It's been said that the average man thinks about sex every seven seconds.

It's also been said that this is nothing but a phallusy. Er, fallacy. (You didn't really think that women preferred shopping to fucking, did you?)

You know, I've always had my suspicions. About the seven-second span, I mean. I've always thought of it as an urban legend, a myth that gives men yet another excuse to be prurient and promiscuous without compunction. Nearly all of my exes have confirmed this theory, though none have lent it more credibility than my current boyfriend.

I don't know what it is, but sex simply doesn't appeal to Jesse. Don't get me wrong. He performs his...manly duties, if you will, but with all the enthusiasm of a patient getting a lumbar puncture. (What I wouldn't give to get a fraction of the action you see on all those medical melodramas.) With Jesse, it's consistently wham-bam-when-will-this-be-over-ma'am? He just goes through the motions, treating sex like an onus, a sacrifice he has to make for the sake of our relationship.

I know what you're thinking. You're thinking that my guy's not attracted to me anymore. You're thinking that I need to spruce myself up—make my teeth a little whiter, my hair a little lighter, my waist a little tighter. I'm sure you mean well, but let's ditch the double standard, shall we? Let's focus on what we can do to erectify the problem. Er, rectify. (I'll stop, I'll stop, I promise.)

Curiously, while Jesse is hardly the amorous type, he's downright exuberant when it comes to expressing affection. He's the first to reach for my hand when we're out in public, the first to kiss me good morning, good-bye, and goodnight. He says, "You're lovely," and "I love you," and "How was your day, love?"

But sometimes—and pardon my appropriation of lugubrious song lyrics; I'm trying to illustrate a point here—love just ain't enough. Sometimes I need a little lust to go with my love; I want Jesse all hot and bothered, panting and pulsating and perspiring, his hands greedy and his cock needy and... Well, you're a woman. You understand the pleasure principle.

You know, that's exactly what I need right now. Understanding, I mean. I need to vent and lament this conundrum with my flock of female friends.

Lindsay studies me, her shoulders hunched, her brows bunched up like a hair scrunchie. "What are you bitching about, Marnie? I should have your problems," she snivels, for Lindsay is a product of the me generation. "My boyfriend is insufferable. And insatiable. He's insufferably insatiable, that's what he is. I think there's something seriously wrong with his"—she pauses, trying to decide on an appropriate euphemism—"little soldier. It's like some sort of maniacal jackhammer. I say give the man his walking papers and be done with it."

On the opposite side of the booth, Jocelyn shakes her head slowly, pitying her prissy, prudish friend. "Pay no attention to her, Marnie," she counsels, sprinkling sugar into her coffee. "It's dysfunction junction, I'll bet you anything. You know what he needs, don't you? The little blue diamonds. It's been well-established that diamonds are a girl's best friend." Now would probably be a bad time to point out that Jocelyn is an advice columnist. I still haven't decided whether she's underqualified or overqualified for the job.

"I didn't say he couldn't perform," I remind her. "I said—"

"Maybe he's gay," Paula interjects, spreading a schmear of cream cheese onto her bagel. "Why don't you strap on a strap-on and see if that gets his juices pumping?" she suggests, because the world according to Paula is nothing more than a cramped, colossal closet.

It occurs to me then that the glass of orange juice sitting in front of me is no longer half-full but half-empty. I push it away. My temples throb, my unmitigated frustration having manifested itself in the form of a migraine. I'm about to utter the official declaration of defeat—check, please!—when Bethany, the only one of my friends who prefers to be seen but not heard, offers her assessment of the situation.

"Maybe," Bethany begins, taking the tentative approach, "Jesse does enjoy sex, just not the kind of sex you're having. Maybe it's too tame for him, too...vanilla." She pauses, concentrating on scraping the charred surface of her toast. "I'm sure he likes vanilla just fine, but maybe he likes variety, too. Maybe he wants to...sample other flavors every once in a while, change it up a bit. You told me once that Jesse is the first guy you've dated who has no interest in, um, in pornography, right?"

It's true. Jesse isn't a sleaze-and-please type of guy. None of it stimulates him. Not if it's captured on celluloid, not if it's circulating in cyberspace. He flinches at the sight of women in the throes of faux ecstasy, winces at the plight of vixens immersed in violence, voyeurism and vulgarity. Even sapphic smut fails to whet Jesse's appetite. Soft core or hard core, it's all an eyesore to him.

"Maybe," Bethany surmises, coaxing a strawberry onto her spoon, "it's not disgust that he feels when he looks at those kinds of images. Maybe it's envy."

Envy.

Envy?

Envy!

Finally, a gem of advice amongst cubic zirconias.

"Perhaps," Bethany continues, a welcome respite from her maybes, "he hasn't told you how he feels because he's worried you'll think he's depraved."

That's just like Jesse, worried I'll think he's depraved. He doesn't even curse in my presence, because he's afraid he'll offend my delicate sensibilities.

"You're a sex-life saver," I gush, giving Bethany a much-deserved squeeze and thank-you.

Well, ladies, it looks like the old in-and-out has gotten old and is on its way out. I need to start thinking outside the box. To be more precise, I need to start thinking outside my box. (Hey, when I get horny, I get corny, what can I say?)

I can say that I'm confident I can fix this.

Yes.

Just give me a week.

And a whip.

Come Monday morning, I am up and at him bright and early, taking advantage of the fact that Jesse is a heavy sleeper. Please—Bob and Carol and Ted and Alice could be participating in an orgy right there on the bed and my guy wouldn't even stir. I flip back the covers, revealing the slumbering form nestled in the sheets. I take a moment to scrutinize Jesse. His hair, trimmed in woodruff blond locks, tickles his eyelashes, his lids concealing the hazel hue of his irises. His body, slim yet sturdy, is swaddled in briefs and an undershirt, both white, the color of virtue and purity.

I shift Jesse onto his side and proceed to strip him from the waist down, as if peeling the wrapper off a lollipop. My eyes descend to his belly, to the flaccid phallus beneath his navel. It dangles there, idly, like an earring. Be patient, I instruct myself. Good things come to those who wait. Opting to leave his undershirt on—a heavy sleeper is anything but lightweight—I nudge Jesse back into a prone position. This has the desirable effect of baring his hind quarters, and I decide to partake in a little voyeurism. Jesse's backside is his best side, sinewy and sinuous, like a hothouse tomato. Ripe for the beating.

I leave Jesse's side momentarily to retrieve the restraints. (Though I don't anticipate a struggle, it never hurts to be prepared.) Before settling on bondage tape, I considered a variety of manacles and fetters: handcuffs, scarves, ropes. Handcuffs are best left to novices and magicians and officers of the law. Scarves and ropes, on the other hand, well, let's just say that my stomach twists into knots at the thought of having to remove them. (I'd be lucky to last five minutes alone in the wilderness.)

As I snip the powder blue tape into strips, I begin to feel giddy, refulgent with rapture. There's something to be said about this whole power-trip concept, I muse, winding the clingy material around Jesse's wrists and ankles, tethering him to the bedposts. With his arms and legs splayed, he looks like he is in the middle of a cartwheel.

When I have secured all of the necessary appendages, I go

and fetch the whip. Eschewing simplicity, I have chosen a rather unique implement. I could have picked a regular old riding crop or a cat-o'-nine-tails, something a little more classic. You know, tried and true, designed to leave its victim black-and-blue. But those instruments are a little too insipid for my tastes.

So I'm going to give Jesse a hand. No, I'm not being facetious. I selected this switch specifically for its sentimental value. The flogging end of the whip is shaped like a hand, the fingers stubby and pudgy, and it reminds me of the Mickey Mouse glove that Jesse and I bought as a souvenir on our first vacation as a couple. I love the illusion that it conveys. How could anything so cute and cartoonish possibly inflict pain and punishment?

As I flex the whip between my fingers, I ponder the shades of the bruises. The contusions will emerge in hues of pink: pink like a pink Cadillac, pink like a pencil eraser, pink like pink lemonade, pink like the Pink Panther. As the whipping increases in vigor and velocity, those hues of pink will shade into tones of red: red like a stop sign, red like a Valentine heart, red like Dorothy's ruby red slippers, red like Mickey's shorts and Minnie's dress, red like—

"Marnie, what are these?"

I look up from the lash to see Jesse twisting his wrists and ankles against the restraints.

"These, my dear," I reply, tapping one with the whip, "are the ties that bind."

Jesse bristles, but the flush of color in his face belies his discomfort. "What are we doing?" he inquires, his choice of pronoun conveying his desire to participate.

I tilt my head, bending the shaft of the whip until it is curved like a semi-erect cock. "Well, now, you tell me, Jesse," I reply, and flutter my lashes, my eyes stretched wide.

"Why, Grandma, what big eyes you have," Jesse remarks. His

voice has a quavering quality to it, a feeble attempt at sounding petrified.

"All the better to see through you with, my dear," I counter, climbing onto the bed and settling down beside his exposed rear end. "I have to admit, sweetie, I never thought of you as the kinky kind."

"I'm not," he insists, denying it with the movement of his lips but confirming it with the movement of his hips.

"Oh, you are," I insist, the Mickey Mouse hand poised above his backside. "No ifs, ands or butts about it."

Jesse cranes his neck, peering over his shoulder at the switch in my hand. His eyes narrow as he inspects the instrument. "That looks like—"

"I know. Isn't it precious?"

Jesse chuckles, tugging on his tethers, but he isn't resisting. "I doubt it'll do much damage," he surmises. "You're almost better off using a flyswatter."

"Well, we'll soon find out just how big a wallop it packs, now, won't we?" I murmur, the hand coming closer.

"I guess we—"

I deliver the first blow, the firm black vinyl of the crop connecting with the taut white flesh of his ass. Jesse yelps, sounding at once pained and pleased. I take my time, allowing several seconds to lapse between blows. During this brief period of recovery, I watch closely for signs that the throbbing has begun to subside, and when his breathing becomes more effortless, when the muscles in his ass become more relaxed, the switch strikes again.

With each whack, Jesse emits a whine-cum-whimper, like windshield wipers squeaking against the glass. I watch as his backside, now sporting a crimson complexion, jumps and jiggles on impact.

Jesse wails as I whale him, the bruises invading his flesh, spreading like spilled red wine. I can feel my heart thudding inside my chest, beating in time to the cadence of the thwacks. My skin smolders, tingles surging through my body, zipping back and forth from neuron to neuron, yet always returning to my pussy. The intensity of the whipping escalates, until the flogging becomes fast and fervent and frenzied.

"Tape."

Instantly, I stop, the hand hovering over his ass. "What?" I mutter, bewildered.

"Tape," Jesse repeats, his voice raspy. "Please take off the tape."

Please? Did he just say please? I almost laugh out loud. Even when he's ensnared in the throes of passion, Jesse still minds his manners.

I release him from his restraints, carefully peeling the self-clinging tape away from his skin. When he is free from captivity, Jesse turns onto his back. I see him cringe in distress as his bottom makes contact with the mattress.

"It seems so much harder now," he observes, squirming against the sheets.

My gaze gravitates to his groin. "The same goes for you," I remark, my mouth watering until it is nearly as moist as my pussy. The spiked organ looks positively regal, and I revel in its beauty, in the corpulence of his cock. Precum drizzles down his shaft, like an icicle melting in the heat of the sun.

Jesse beckons me to the bed and I shuck my panties midstride. "Do you want to be on top?" I offer, concerned about his comfort.

"No, thank you," Jesse declines, embracing my waist.

I straddle his thighs and settle onto his lap, welcoming him into the confines of my cunt. I can feel my pussy expanding to accommodate the length and girth of him. My torso undulates, grinding gently and gradually, his cock sloshing within the wetness of my pussy. His eyelids languish, the only part of his body that is flaccid at the moment.

Jesse's hand treks along my abdomen, and I tremble as his fingers venture between my legs. His palm drifts across the shroud of curls covering my pussy, en route to my clit. Instinctively, I pick up the pace. Our breathing becomes emphatic, erratic, spurts of sound slithering through our lips as the friction builds swiftly to a frisson.

The time between our climaxes is immeasurable, infinitesimal. The ardor of Jesse's arousal, the rapidity of our lovemaking, activates a geyser of jism. It mixes with my juices, creating a euphoric elixir and propelling me to orgasm as well.

Afterward, we curl up together, the Mickey whip nestled between us. "Jesse, I don't think you're depraved," I say, anticipating the question before he can ask it.

Jesse simpers. I smile. "How did you know that I would... enjoy that?" he wonders, stroking my hand as I stroke his bottom.

"I didn't," I admit. "Bethany did."

"That's a very unusual case of woman's intuition," Jesse remarks, blushing profusely.

"I'll elaborate when I'm not so exhausted," I offer, tucking the duvet under my chin. "Would you like to do this again sometime? Say, tomorrow? And again every day for a week? And then... Well, I think after that, Mickey's got some vacation time coming to him."

Jesse nods, his enthusiasm bordering on fanaticism. "Yes, please. And...thank you."

My fingers curl around his hip. "What are the magic words?"

"I said please and thank you," Jesse protests, his mouth drooping into a pout.

I make a mental note to treat Bethany to a day at the spa, because I can't think of anyone more deserving. "No, sweetie," I insist, a smirk sneaking onto my lips. "The magic words are *please* and *spank you.*"

A LITTLE PUSH

Felix D'Angelo

How had I let her talk me into this?

As "Bolero" pounded slowly toward its climax, Carrie stretched out on the bed with legs spread wide, thick pillows tucked under her hips. This position tipped her perfect ass upward at just the perfect angle. Her asshole, glistening and virgin, beckoned to me between her slightly spread pale pink cheeks. It was wet from my spittle; I'd spent the last forty-five minutes rimming the hell out of her while I finger-fucked her senseless, two orgasms' worth; that's why immediately under her ass her cunt was pink and dripping. There'd been no lube so far, just my tongue, buried deep in her ass. I snapped on the glove, popped the top on the tube of Think Anal lube and saw Carrie's pretty face regarding me over her slim shoulder. She reached back and gently parted her asscheeks, displaying her asshole to me shamelessly.

"You're not having second thoughts, are you?" she purred wickedly. "Come on, babe...you know you want it."

Did I? I wasn't sure, but I did know I couldn't resist it. The taste of her musky ass filled my mouth; with each stroke of my tongue my cock had throbbed harder, my lust for her tight virgin asshole growing. I locked eyes with my girlfriend as I glorped lube out onto my fingers and began to massage it into her asshole.

She was snug, even with the long strokes of my tongue; by the end there, my tongue had been deep into her back door. But just one finger made her gasp, and the snug cinch of the sphincter around my middle finger sent a wave of hot desire through my body; Christ, I wanted to fuck Carrie's ass so bad....

I withdrew my finger.

"I can't," I said.

"Is it the music?" she asked. "I've got David Bowie—"

"No, I just can't," I said.

"Can't?" pouted Carrie. "But my ass, Jack...my virgin tight ass..." she wriggled her perfect apple cheeks back and forth, clenching, releasing, slipping one middle finger down to caress her crack; then she whimpered as she began finger-fucking her own ass, and—

"Fuck it," I said, and lurched forward.

"My sentiments exactly," said Carrie, letting me nudge her finger out of the way to replace it with my own, rubber clad, slick with lube, gently working her open, quickly replaced by a second, which made her gasp and hiss and whimper, rocking her hips as she pushed herself onto me.

"Cock, baby," she moaned softly. "I want your cock."

"We're supposed to go slow."

"Then I want your cock slowly."

"You're getting it." It wasn't so much that I worried about hurting my girlfriend—I did, but then Carrie was very much capable of letting me know if something didn't feel right. Quite the contrary; I worried—no, best not to think about that now.

I worked in a third finger, and Carrie pressed back onto my hand, sliding rhythmically back and forth like she was giving a lap dance. Her muscles clenched tight and I let her relax as I worked all three fingers in deeply, till they formed a little heart shape, holding her asshole open stretched and eager.

"I think I'm ready," she said. "I want your cock."

"Do you want a condom?"

She made a disdainful noise and a sour face. "Fuck, no. We're tested, remember?"

"Wouldn't it be smoother?"

"Than your cock? I don't think so," she said. Then, deep, hot, in a low, sensuous purr: "I want your cock naked inside me, Jack...put it in already, will you?"

I leaned firmly forward. My cock, still wet from her spit, slid easily into my grasp and as my fingers went softly slurping out, I felt the snugness of her asshole up against my naked cockhead.

"Breath in deep, and then—FUCK!"

She gave a little push back onto me, whimpering. My cockhead popped in, and she made a bestial sound as she pushed her snug ass slowly down my shaft, looking over her shoulder to make sure I saw the rapturous expression on her face as she took me into her virgin hole. "You were saying?" she asked me.

My eyes rolled back into my head. I fumbled the wet rubber glove off of my hand and threw it on the floor. I let her snuggle down onto me and gradually acclimate herself to the bulk in her hole. She started clenching-releasing, clenching-releasing, each time relaxing more. I felt a quick rubbing and realized she was stroking her clit fervently, periodically dipping two fingers into her cunt. When she did that I could feel her ass tighten, even feel the pressure, a little, of her fingertips against my cock.

"Bolero" rose in mounting rhythmic fuck-sounds; things were getting serious.

"All right," she said softly. "Now fuck me."

I started slowly, gradually, working in and out inch by inch, shocked at how different ass felt than cunt. As I came partway out, she smeared lube on me with the hand that wasn't on her pussy. Then, "Harder," she begged, and I gave it my best, thrusting deeper until her asshole was around the very base of my cock shaft, then drawing back until I almost slipped out. I leaned forward, pinning her down so I could get more leverage with my hips. I started thrusting, slowly then quicker, quicker, quicker, as Carrie squirmed under me, the thrusts getting easier with each stroke. I was close—fucking close, fast as hell since her ass was so tight and the turn-on was tangible.

"Um—I'm ready—you want it—?"

"Yeah, yeah, up my ass," she said irritably, breathlessly. "Come in my ass. Wait—not—not yet—"

She rubbed harder, almost violently; I struggled to hold still while she went at it. Then she let out a low keening wail and her ass tightened rhythmically; she gave a yelp of surprise as my cock popped smoothly out.

"Back in," she pleaded, and I worked it back in. Her ass was still spasming as I drove deep inside her and started thrusting. In another moment I started to come, giving a girly little whimper as I gripped her hair and pounded her ass. Borne into the bed by my weight, Carrie lifted her ass to meet my thrusts. Her ass went slick with my semen. "Bolero" screamed its final whining cacophony, yowling to its violent end.

I grunted. I finished. Her cunt and ass were still twitching, little "Oooh" sounds escaping her lips as she felt the afterglow of her orgasm. After a time I rolled off of her, lay on my back panting. Affectionately, she snuggled on top of me.

The CD started again: *Bum, da da da, ba da da da da da bum da da da…* Christ, was Carrie really going to tell people for the rest of her life that she lost her anal virginity to the strains of "Bolero"? It seemed like adding insult to perversion, though I admitted the rhythm was mildly soothing, however much my asscheeks were clenching.

She must have read worry on my face; she gave a broad grin, giggling evilly.

"Oh, don't be nervous, baby.... It was my first time, and tomorrow it'll be your first time." She laughed.

"Tomorrow? I thought we said 'some time.'"

Carrie gave me her best innocent face. "Come on, baby, you're not going to make me wait, are you? I didn't make you wait... Well, not very long, at least. Please?"

"All right," I said. "I guess so. If you're sure it won't—"

"No, it doesn't hurt, baby. And you know you want it. Or at least you know you're curious about it."

I shrugged, trying to play cool.

"Don't give me that," said Carrie, and kissed my chest wetly, with lots of tongue. "Of course," she breathed, "I would never want to do anything to you that you weren't totally into. You can always puss out...and go back on your word...and get your girlfriend to give up her ass, but be chicken to—"

"Forget it," I said. "I'll make good on our bargain."

Carrie gave her most mischievous grin, her whole body seeming to hum with excitement from the prospect—or maybe it was that she had just gotten fucked in the ass.

"Would you...show me?" I asked.

Carrie looked surprised.

"I mean, you already bought it, right?"

"Yeah, but I thought... I figured we'd wait until..."

"Please? I'm just curious."

"Sure," she said. "That's hot. You don't want..."

"Tonight? No. I just... I'd just like to see it."

"Maybe suck it a little?"

"Suck it? That's weird." I grinned.

"Men," she said, smiling. "All right. Fashion show. You wait right here, baby." She got out of bed.

Carrie's campus apartment has shared baths between each pair of bedrooms. She seized a black plastic bag with a dog-collar logo from the decrepit particleboard laminate wardrobe, and paused at the door.

"Don't go anywhere," she said, and shut the door behind her.

I rolled over onto my belly, felt immediately self-conscious—since that put my ass in a direct line of sight from the bathroom door. I rolled onto my side. My cock ached from the fuck; Carrie's asshole was tight, and the heat of my first anal fuck was as hot as the excitement of taking Carrie's anal virginity.

But with Carrie, nothing is ever simple; what's more, she's fantastically persuasive. When I'd made my thoughts clear—that anal sex was fucking hot, and I couldn't wait to do it—she conceived of a bargain. She'd never done it before, but she would. I could be the man to initiate her into the pleasures of back-door love. *If* I'd offer her the same consideration.

Oh, don't get me wrong. I played hard to get. I blushed, hemmed and hawed, wasn't sure I could do that—still wasn't. But the night she suggested it, *fuck!* how my cock swelled and throbbed.

Ever since then—three weeks, now, long enough for her to buy a strap-on and me to read three neurotic books on safety, tips, guidelines and precautious—I'd been half-obsessed, careening wildly between imagining Carrie's tight ass snugged around my slick cock, and her cock, buried deep—Motherfucker, I couldn't even think about it without popping a hard-on, which I did, and before I knew it I was stroking—my cock wet with lube and Carrie's ass, my ass feeling suddenly hungry.

My cock was sore, the tip stung slightly, and still I fucking stroked it, reaching back to touch my own firm cheeks—good god, was I a pervert?

"Baby?"

"Patience!" she cried back. "This thing's not sweats and a goddamn T-shirt, Jackie boy, and it's not attached to me!"

"Sorry," I said meekly.

I went back to stroking gently, almost hyperventilating. I'd decided: why put off until tomorrow... My cheeks clenched. I squirted lube and reached back there.

I was tight—tighter than Carrie. Two fingers took some work to get in. Three was almost impossible at first. Four—well, once I'd done three, four seemed like an awesome idea, and then I was fucking, wetly, eyes rolling back into my head. I was clean, I'd seen to that, knowing this was a possibility—since my vivid fantasies had me doing just this, fucking Carrie's ass and then...oh, fuck. I thrust fingers deeper, pumped my cock, felt my asshole relaxing....

"Bolero" was pulsing louder.

"Baby?"

"Goddamn buckles! Just a minute."

I watched, panting and stroking, as I waited for the door to open. The CD had started over before it did; she sashayed out adorned and gussied; I stared gape-mouthed as her eyes flickered over my lube-slick cock. I'd slid my fingers out of my ass and was caressing my prick with both hands.

"You like, I guess," she said.

"Those boots!"

"They match the harness," said Carrie.

"Expensive?"

"I hope my dad doesn't check his credit card statement this month. I'm just saying."

Her hand went gliding slowly down her body, fingers nuzzling her tits, her belly, then circling the big flesh-colored cock jutting out of her harness.

"It looks so real," I said, sitting up on the edge of the bed.

She stroked her cock as she made her way across the bedroom, spike-heeled patent-leather knee-high monstrosities spearing lube packets and discarded comic books. "I thought...you know, smooth, purple or something, that'll be less, er, real. But then...you know, there's something hot about how it looks like a real cock. Isn't that kind of hot, Jackie? Jackie? Oh, my..."

My mouth engulfed the head of her cock and I felt a powerful charge of excitement go through me. Oh, fuck, I was actually going to do this.

I took her cock down easily to the back of my throat, my head bobbing up and down as she ground her hips forward. It wasn't just the anal sex books I'd learned from; never having seen her strap-on before, I had already gauged the angle of the base. Line drawings can be so helpful. I calculated its proximity to Carrie's clit, which, let's be frank, I knew the location of pretty goddamn well. I started sucking, hand around the lower portion of the shaft, got the base of the dildo tight against Carrie's clit, and—drunken sailors never moaned so loud when street whores' throats went tight around their cock shafts.

I felt wires, but didn't think twice about them; I was too fixated on sucking Carrie's strap-on. I started working fervently, my hand around Carrie's firm body, gripping that perfect ass I'd just fucked and pulling it hard against me, hard cock down my throat. She held me, her crotch against my face, her hands gripping my hair as I struggled to keep her down as deep inside me as I could.

"I've been practicing," I rasped when I came up for air, which was not for a good long time.

"You little whore," she said. "You've been playing hard to get."

Don't make me beg, I thought. *I'll puss out.*

But she didn't, she just let me suck and suck, my own cock throbbing, until I looked up at her with big wide eyes and she gave me a little push onto the bed.

"On your knees, lover."

"But you said tomorrow," I whined with a vague smile, even as I obeyed her push and got on my hands and knees.

She got behind me.

"But your ass says now, now, now." She didn't bother with a glove; she'd trimmed her nails short. I'd left the lube half-opened, leaking goo onto her pillow. I groped after it, handed it over my shoulder, and felt a cool slick stream joining the thick coat that still greased my asshole.

I made girly sounds as her fingers worked into me. Carrie's fingers were considerably narrower than mine; she got two, three, four in there, easy as pie, and then before I even knew it a shockingly realistic dildo was up against my asshole and my eyes went wide with momentary fright.

Then with a little push, my girlfriend entered me. The cock was not enormous, but she had not gone mini, either; it was healthy in its thickness and my asshole opened slowly. But she got it in, a little push, another, another, another, sliding easily back and forth until Carrie's thighs settled tight against mine and I could feel her cock all the way in my ass.

Between pulses of "Bolero," I heard a click, then a buzz; felt a throbbing. Carrie moaned.

Holy fuck. She was going to fuck me till she came. Just like a real assfucker—just like me, in her ass, that gorgeous ass flexing and releasing with every thrust of her cock into me, an ass filled with my come—

I started stroking.

Carrie moaned louder, one hand steadying herself on the small of my back, the other working the wired vibrator, varying its pulses as she teased herself to climax and the music built louder and louder.

Then she came, her thick cock pounding deep inside of me, her thrusts matched to the spasmodic jerks of her orgasm, shuddering pleasure raging through her cock and into my ass. The assfuck gave every possible hint of realism except her cum pumping—and I provided that part, hot streams shooting over my hand and arm, soaking the bed as I cried out. Whether she came first or I did, I really don't know, because she was making noises for a good long time as she drove me down into the bed and bit deep into the flesh of my shoulder and neck, leaving hickeys, I was sure of it. When she was good and done and sated, she switched the vibrator off and I felt the buzz dissipate.

We lay like that through another half-playing of the CD, as Carrie's hot breath ruffled my hair and her fingers caressed my arms.

"Are we even, Jackie baby?"

"I don't know," I said. "You've got a pretty awesome asshole, baby. Maybe a few more times should do it...."

With a little push, I eased her out of me.

DISHPAN HANDS

Jan Darby

As she trudged through the rain from the car to her back door, it occurred to Jane that sometimes she thought she'd be a lot happier as a conscience-free psychopath. She could throw together a bogus expense report without agonizing over which meals she'd really worked through and which she'd enjoyed with friends. She could tell Leanne in accounting that yes, every single thing in the anorectic woman's wardrobe made her look fat. And, best of all, she could strangle her cheating boyfriend. All without a single pang of guilt.

Jane unlocked the door and stepped into the dark mudroom. Replacing the bulb in the overhead fixture had been on Mark's list of household projects for months and months and months. So long, in fact, that she didn't even bother trying the switch. Mark had had plenty of time to do a few projects this past weekend while she'd been out of town on business, but he'd been at a hotel with Leanne, doing her instead of his chores.

The brightness of the adjoining kitchen was just one more

annoying reminder of her ex-boyfriend. He'd apparently forgotten—again—to turn the lights off before he left this morning. He always left a mess behind for her to clean up.

She was too tired to deal with it right now. As she turned toward the stairs to the second-floor bedroom, she heard the sound of splashing water and clinking china. It sounded like someone was in the kitchen, washing dishes.

She peered around the corner, and there, standing at the sink with his back to her, his shirt off, his hands in water up to his elbows, was Mark. The cheating bastard.

He deserved to die, she thought. He really did. But she was sane and she couldn't kill him in cold blood. Especially not while he had his back to her.

She'd always thought his back was spectacular. Jane watched the play of muscles until her gaze caught on the tiny mole beneath one shoulder blade, right where she used to cling to him while coming.

He was damned good in bed, which only made her wish, once again, that she were insane. Then, she might be able to convince herself that the physical pleasure was enough. It was so tempting. But she couldn't give in. She was nothing if not rational.

She could indulge in a little righteous indignation, though, and her voice reflected her annoyance. "What are you doing here?"

He didn't turn around, simply continued what he was doing. "I'm washing the breakfast dishes."

"I can see that." Her fists clenched, and she hid them behind her. She was not going to kill him, no matter how much he deserved it. "You aren't supposed to be here. You were supposed to leave this morning. Permanently."

He shrugged, setting his lovely back muscles into play again.

"There was work to do here first. I owe you that much."

She tore her gaze away from the skin she knew so well. The skin that Leanne now knew better than she should. "A warehouse full of clean dishes wouldn't settle your debt."

"It's a start." He tossed a towel over his shoulder. "My dad always told me that women love a man who'll do household chores. He'd say, 'All the domestic violence these days, and you never hear about even one man who died while washing dishes. Remember that, and you'll live happily ever after.'"

She forced herself to look away from his appealing back and stare at the floor, where puddles were forming around Mark's feet from his exuberant rinsing. He couldn't even clean things without making a mess. "Your father died of a heart attack while cheating on your mother."

"He was always better at giving advice than taking it." Mark turned around to face her. "And I didn't cheat on you with Leanne."

"Why would she lie about it?"

"Because she's jealous of you, and she wants you to be as miserable as she is." He pulled the towel off his shoulder and began drying a cereal bowl. "She knows your itinerary from reviewing your expense reports, so she knows how much you've been on the road lately, and it wouldn't take much to guess that it was affecting our relationship."

"Our relationship did suffer," she said. "But it was surviving until you broke it."

He shook his head. "I didn't cheat on you. She played you."

He sounded so disappointed, she almost believed him. Almost. "The house was a wreck when I got home on Sunday. You certainly weren't here washing dishes the whole time I was gone."

"I wish I had been." He put down the first cereal bowl and

picked up another. "It was stupid. I meant to do some stuff around here, but I lost track of time playing video games."

She'd complained often enough about the hours and hours he wasted with his stupid games, but he couldn't have thought they were worse than cheating on her. "Why didn't you tell me that yesterday?"

"You were too angry to listen," he said. "I was waiting for you to calm down."

She'd been so angry last night, it wouldn't have taken much to push her over the edge of sanity. She'd known it too, and had sensibly locked herself in the bedroom until the rage dissipated. Toward morning, she'd begun to consider her own contributions to the failure of their relationship. She wasn't entirely blameless. She owed him a chance to explain. "I'm calm now. What did you want to tell me?"

"I didn't do what she claimed," he said. "And I'm sorry."

"If you weren't with Leanne, there's nothing to be sorry for."

"I didn't cheat on you, but I did fail you," he said. "I've let you do all the hard work the whole time we've been together. That's what I have to apologize for."

"I suppose it wasn't really about Leanne," Jane said. "She was just an excuse. I'm tired of doing all the work around here, and even more tired of trying to get you to help."

"I did this morning's dishes."

"That's a start," she said. "How much longer are you willing to do them?"

"Forever."

Jane might believe him about Leanne, but some things would never change. Not for long. "You'll get dishpan hands."

"Never." Mark raised his hands in front of him and wiggled his yellow-gloved fingers at her. "My dad taught me all about latex. In all its forms."

She looked at the puddles on the floor, trying not to give in to the amusement. She wanted to kill him, after all, not laugh with him. The relationship was over, and he had to leave.

"One more chance," he said, correctly reading her uncertainty. "Tell me what you want, and I'll do it. Anything."

Having an eager, capable man at her beck and call might have been another woman's fantasy, Jane thought, but it wasn't hers. "I want you to do things without being told. I'm tired of being in charge."

He concentrated on removing first one latex glove and then the other, a thoughtful expression on his face. "You want me to show some initiative?"

"Not just some," she said. "All. I don't want to make any more decisions for us. I want you to make them. Every single one of them. It's your turn."

He tossed the gloves into the sink. "You wouldn't last two minutes without taking over."

Expecting Mark to act responsibly was even more insane than plotting to kill him, she thought, but at least she wouldn't end up in jail. "If you can change your behavior, I can change mine."

He leaned against the sink for several thoughtful moments before holding out his arms to her. "Come here."

"I'm too tired for games."

He dropped his hands to his sides. "Two seconds. You didn't even last two seconds with me in charge."

He was serious, she realized. He was willing to take on some responsibility, if she would just let him. "I'm sorry."

He raised his arms again, and this time she moved into his embrace, snuggling into the damp, dish-soapy skin of his chest. His chin dropped to rest on the top of her head. "Thank you."

He wrapped his arms around her waist and held her close, and she couldn't help thinking that she'd known him to stare into space—or a video screen—for hours, doing absolutely nothing worthwhile. If it were up to him, they might spend the next forty-eight hours standing here, just hugging in suspended animation. Someone had to say something, get things moving. "Let's go upstairs."

He raised his head. "Ninety seconds this time. You're getting better."

Not really, she thought. She was getting worse, inching closer to the insanity she envied, because she actually felt guilty for making an obvious little suggestion. She willed herself to relax. "I can do this. Really."

"I'll be expecting a lot from you."

That was only fair. She'd always demanded a lot from him. She could handle anything except the total responsibility she'd borne until now. She nodded against his chest. "Whatever you want."

He picked her up and seated her on the marble-topped kitchen island, slick with soap and water splatters from his dishwashing. "I want you."

And she wanted him. Physically, at least. They'd never had any problems with sex.

She started to unbutton her blouse, but he placed his hand over hers. "I didn't tell you to do that, did I?"

"I thought it was what you wanted."

"Don't think for me," he said. "Just do what I tell you."

"I was trying to help."

"I'm a big boy." He brushed her hands away and took over undressing her. "I can do it myself."

He parted the fabric slowly, stopping between each undone button to brush his thumbs over the newly exposed skin: the upper slopes of her breasts, then each of her ribs and finally her bellybutton.

It felt nice, but it wasn't the hot, frantic make-up sex she craved. He was supposed to tear off her clothes and kiss her wildly and then fuck her insensible. "Are you sure you don't want some help?"

"I'm sure." He slipped the blouse off her shoulders and kissed her neck.

"This is going to take all night."

"That's the idea." He continued with all the single-minded concentration he usually reserved for video games. He undid her pants zipper and slid his hand inside. Between kisses, he said, "I want to play with you all night."

"We can't," she said, still a little irritated with him. "I have to get some sleep before I go to the office tomorrow."

"Maybe."

That was going too far, she thought, and she was about to complain when he found her clit and squeezed it. She could spare him a little time. They'd both be finished in a few minutes, anyway, so there was no point in worrying about an all-nighter. She lay back on the marble-topped island, letting him remove her remaining clothes and toss them on the floor.

He took a step back, cupped one elbow in the other hand and stared at her naked pussy. "This is where the decisions become so difficult. There are so many possibilities."

"You were doing fine until now," she said. "Just keep doing what you were doing."

"That's for me to decide."

She covered her face with an arm to hide the rolling of her eyes. He couldn't be serious about this.

A moment later, she heard the sound of a stool being dragged over to a spot in front of her. She peered out from behind her arm to see Mark seating himself between her thighs and staring at her.

He looked serious. He wasn't going to take directions from her this time. She was going to have to wait and wonder what he would do next. She didn't want to wait. She wanted it now.

Her hips squirmed demandingly, and he placed one hand on her pussy, holding her still. "I've made a decision."

"Good." She tried to rub against his hand, guiding him by example, but he took his hand away.

"I've wanted to do this forever." He lifted her knees onto his shoulder, her lower legs hanging down his back, and her pussy open to him. "You're always so intent on getting to the end that we never get to enjoy the process." He bent toward her, his tongue teasing its way to her clit and lightly tracing a circle around it.

"We've had oral sex before," she said.

He raised his head. "Not like this. Not with me in charge."

If he wanted to believe that tonight was different, she wasn't going to argue. She needed his mouth on her again. She closed her eyes and wiggled her pelvis at him. "Show me."

"I will," he said. "When I'm ready."

Her eyes popped open. "But I'm ready now."

"I know." He gave her one quick lick, as if to prove that he knew exactly what she wanted and could give it to her—or not—at his own discretion. "I've decided you're going to wait. I like looking at you when you're aroused like this. It's the only time you're not in complete control of yourself."

"I like to be in control." She started to sit up, but then his lips were on her clit again, tugging, making silent promises of the pleasure that would follow eventually. She dropped back onto the chilly marble surface, moaning her pleasure.

"You're going to like being out of control too," he whispered against her skin. "Totally, screamingly out of control."

"I'm not like that."

"You can be." He sucked her until her brain melted, and the concept of control no longer made any sense, and then he raised his head. "Not yet."

"What?" She blinked. "You can't stop now."

"You gave me the right to do anything I choose," he said. "I choose to stop now and watch you cool down a little."

"I don't want to cool down," she said. "I want to come. I want you to suck me again."

"I know," he said. "And I will. When I'm ready."

She groaned in frustration. "How can I make you ready?"

"You can't," he said. "I get to decide."

He'd always fucked her exactly the way she wanted it. Why had she ever thought they needed to change? "Never mind what I said before. You don't have to take on any responsibility. I like being in charge."

"No," he said with more determination than she'd ever heard from him. "That's your pussy talking, not your brain. We're doing this my way, my rules, my timetable."

He meant it, she thought. He was going to make her wait, possibly all night, just to prove he could play this game to the end. "What if it doesn't work?"

"It will work just fine." He tweaked her clit between two fingers. "See?"

She gasped, startled by the intensity of the unexpected little touch, as if she could feel each ridge of his fingerprint as it passed over her skin.

"Perhaps I can give you a little more." He rubbed her gently, and, much as she wanted him to press harder and faster, she knew that saying so would only make him stop, and anything was better than that. She couldn't help squirming, though, and as soon as she did, he stopped.

He couldn't leave her like this. He wouldn't leave her like this. She trusted him. All she had to do was wait.

She'd never realized how hard it was to wait, to be the one who listened, the one who obeyed. A frustrated little cry escaped her, but she didn't let any words form. Nothing that he might consider to be an order. Not even a demand or a plea. She couldn't stop her thoughts, though: *Please, please, please; now, now, now.*

A few thousand silent nows passed. Without warning, he resumed rubbing her clit. Grateful for any contact, she didn't complain that his touch, more erratic and tentative than she was used to, missed as much as it hit. He needed to do it his way, and she needed to let him.

"I don't want this to end," he said, even as he settled into a surer rhythm, making the end inevitable.

She knew he didn't expect an answer, and, in any event, she was beyond words. She waited, enjoying the pleasure he gave her, half believing that he could make it last forever.

"The longer I can make you wait," he said, keeping her at the exact same level of need, "the better the release will be."

She moaned contentedly.

"On the other hand," he said, increasing the pressure slightly, "if you come now, without me, I can watch you come, and then we can start all over again."

This amazing feeling couldn't last forever, she knew, and she was growing more anxious. Her entire body was shaking.

"You can't wait any longer, can you?" he said.

His words barely made sense, and she couldn't speak. She couldn't do anything, except keen with need.

"Next time," he said. "Next time, we'll both know what to expect, and I'll be able to tease you all night long. All you have to do is trust me to do the right thing for both of us." He bent his head to demonstrate the sureness of his tongue, and she ceded what little remained of her self-control, screaming with the pleasure he gave her.

The sun was still shining when Jane scurried into the house an hour early on Friday afternoon. She didn't need to turn on the overhead light of the mudroom to see where she was going, but she flipped the switch anyway. Barely noticeable against the daylight, the newly changed bulb glowed.

As she passed the stairs, she could hear the sound of splashing in the kitchen. She peered around the corner, and there, standing at the sink with his back to her, his shirt off, his hands in the water up to the elbows, was Mark.

"Can I help?" she said, enjoying the display of startled muscles contracting across his spectacular back.

"Not with the dishes." He turned off the faucet and placed the freshly rinsed skillet in the rack to dry. "They're done."

"Anything else?"

He pulled off his yellow gloves. "I'm sure I'll think of something."

"Whatever you want. You're in charge."

"The house is a mess," he said, watching her closely. "And I spent the day playing video games."

He was testing her, she knew, goading her into taking charge. A week ago, she'd have been making lists and dividing up the projects. Today, she wasn't even tempted. The house, the mess, the priorities—they were all Mark's responsibility now and he could keep them.

"Whatever." She tugged off her suit jacket and tossed it on the top of the island where he'd first shown her just how responsible and decisive he could be.

"Let's get to work." He grabbed his latex gloves. "Upstairs. Now."

He herded her past the bed and into the adjoining master bathroom. It was Mark's favorite room in the house, the only significant project he'd actually finished since moving in with her. He'd completely redone the space, adding a walk-in shower big enough for them to share.

"You might as well strip, so your clothes won't get wet while we work." He gestured at his own bare chest, and then began removing his jeans. "It's more efficient this way."

Reasonably certain that he wasn't going to do any real scrubbing once they were both naked, Jane quickly undressed, tossing her clothes into the hamper on top of his jeans.

"The shower. Now." Mark handed her one of the natural sea-wool sponges from beside the sink.

"The regular sponges are under the sink," she said. "These are supposed to be used on people, not tiles."

"I know what I'm doing." He turned on the water and backed her into the shower, all the way to the built-in bench along the far wall.

"Have a seat."

She resisted until he said, "Trust me," and she remembered how well the evening had turned out the last time she'd given him free rein.

She sat abruptly.

"I'm getting pretty good at cleaning," he said, slipping on his latex gloves and then turning on the shower faucet. "It's all about patience and perseverance."

"And prioritizing," she said. "Otherwise, it's too easy to run out of time to get things done."

He took the sea sponge from her and drenched it in the water spilling out of the faucet. "I can't work that way. I get more done if I just go with whatever appeals to me at the moment."

The shower stall was filling with steam. "What appeals to you right now?"

"Same as always." Mark squirted shower gel on the sponge. "You."

He started with her neck, skimming the sponge across her skin, leaving a trail of vanilla-scented lather everywhere it touched her. He continued down, working the sponge in a spiral pattern around her breasts, to the nipples, and then down to her belly, making sure that no spot was missed. Finally, he dragged the sponge across her mound and lower, between her legs.

He knelt before her. "Patience and perseverance. Those are the keys to a proper scrubbing." He sponged her pussy, back and forth, as if trying to remove a stubborn stain between her legs. "A man's work is never done."

She closed her eyes and slid down the seat, spreading her legs apart and offering him better access. She heard the impatient snap of the latex gloves as he stripped them off, and then the ragged edges of the sponge found her clit, tickling softly. With each movement of his hand, a different bit of the unevenly shaped sponge touched her, sometimes in one spot, sometimes another, always a surprise.

She craved predictability. And more intensity. "Scrub harder."

The sponge trailed away, down her inner thighs. "Not yet," he said. "This time, we have all night to find out just how long I can keep you aroused before you come."

She opened her eyes. "All night?"

He nodded and held the sponge tantalizingly close to her pussy without quite touching her. "Patience and perseverance."

She closed her eyes and leaned her head against the wall of the shower. Her job was still stressful, Leanne would always annoy her, and the household chores never ended, but they were mere nuisances, fading away beneath Mark's patient, persevering hands.

She lost track of time as he played with her, repeatedly bringing her to the moments of intense pleasure just short of orgasm. Finally, he dropped the sponge and turned a focused stream of water on her clit, sending her through the shivers of pleasure and into exhaustion.

Afterward, he toweled her dry and carried her to their bed. As he tucked her beneath the sheets, she caught a glimpse of the skin on his fingers, all pale and puckered from the prolonged immersion.

"You have amazing hands," Jane said contentedly as she pulled him into bed with her. "Perfect, take-charge, dishpan hands."

MY TURN

Jude Mason

She made the final decision. She always had. Brian gave her choices, and a beautiful, sexy smile, whenever he dreamed up some new game he wanted to try, or was simply horny and wanted her. Of course, if she wanted to play, she'd accept. She nearly always accepted—he had such wonderful ideas and if she wasn't horny to begin with, his suggestions always made her so.

There'd been that time he wanted to take her to a strip club and have her dance. She'd loved the idea and agreed. The spanking he'd given her beforehand made her ass glow brilliantly for the audience. That had been her first taste of exhibitionism but definitely not her last. She'd blossomed in the public eye and her orgasms later had been stupendous. After that, she often wound up in public with some form of disciplinary marks on her body. Or even more exciting, he'd punished her in public. The games got better all the time.

Her face grew warm with a flush and she squirmed, that deliciously squishy feeling spreading from the most female part of her. She loved those exhibitions. She adored Brian.

This time, he'd come up with an even more wicked plan. One that made her shiver with excitement even now. He'd taken her into the den, where they normally began their play, and after waiting for her to strip, sat her at his feet.

Gazing up at him, his tall, dark, good looks and his wicked smile, she wondered what he was up to. The quiet room held their bookcases and the matching leather wingbacked chairs they both loved. It also held the spanking bench and a tall oak cabinet they'd spent months filling with all manner of disciplinary paraphernalia. The rug burned her knees when she moved too quickly, and she stifled a yelp. Shuddering at the adrenaline rush, she smiled her pleasure.

He looked down at her. "Jade, my lovely sweet girl, you make my heart beat faster when you look at me with those eyes." Stroking her long auburn hair, he brought his hand around and cupped her chin with his fingertips. Lifting her face, he forced her to continue looking into his eyes. "Yes, you do take my breath."

Heart beating wildly, she whispered, "Master, what is it?" One of their rules was that she always called him master in this room, when she sat naked at his feet.

"I've got an idea." He smiled. "Something I've been contemplating for some time. Something I'm sure you'll enjoy."

She knew that smile intimately. It was the one he used to warn her, to indicate some new choice was about to be offered.

"Master, what's your idea, if I might ask?"

His eyes took on a glazed faraway look and focused somewhere past her. "I've wondered about how it must feel to be punished. I watch you; see your excitement and how all consuming your orgasms are." Pulling his hand from under her chin, he rose from his chair and went to the window overlooking the garden. The black silk shirt and jeans he wore fit him snuggly, displaying his slenderness and the sleek animal build she adored. He worked hard at keeping himself fit, and it definitely showed.

"You seem to forget everything else in the world; it's all about the sensations you experience and your pleasure." He turned and faced her. "Am I right?"

"Master, Brian, it's all about giving myself to you. You're the one who punishes me, who gives me that pleasure—the freedom to wallow in an orgasm. And, most importantly, I trust you to watch over me, protect me—see that I don't fall or injure myself." She shifted, a little uncomfortably. *Will he refuse me an orgasm next time? Is that what this is all about?*

"Yes, I understand," he said, thoughtfully. He came and crouched in front of her. "What I want to understand is how the pain gives you such an orgasm—so intense, so all encompassing."

Jade thought about it for a moment. How to explain? She knew she had to try. "It's not exactly the pain, Master. You never just flip me over your knee and spank me, there's always something more to it." She dared to look into his eyes unbidden and saw him straining to understand. "It's like foreplay. You touch me, or you tease me in some way. Even when you're actually punishing me, it's never just pain. You seem to know when I'm on the verge of crying out, and just before then, you quit. Then, you slip inside me for a little while, your cock, your fingers, a toy, whichever you want, and work me into a frenzy. Then you stop, altogether, as if you're giving me time to control myself, or to come down from the high. You never let me come with just your cock, though. You mix the pain with it."

He smiled and perhaps caught a glimmer of what she meant. "But when we're in public, you seem to get off even better."

Her face suddenly felt as if it was on fire. “Yes, you know I’m an exhibitionist. I—I don’t know what happens, I just know it excites me like nothing else.” She thought for a moment, and then added, “I said, I trusted you to keep me safe, remember?”

“Yes.”

“Well, that’s part of it too. I can let myself be excited, because I know you’re there. I know you’ll keep me safe.” She became lost in thought, revisiting a particularly hot session they’d had in a nearby town. Brian had taken her to an incredibly posh restaurant. He’d told her to go into the ladies’ room and insert the dildo he’d stashed in her purse. It was one of those remote-control toys, and he’d kept her on the edge of her seat all evening. She’d loved it, and so had he.

Chuckling, Brian slipped his hand along the inside of her right thigh, bringing her back to the present with a lurch. His touch felt cool on her flesh and a shiver raced up her spine. Sliding his fingers higher, he brushed the plump folds of her sex, and drew a gasp from deep inside her. “You’re wet just thinking about it, aren’t you?”

“Yes, just being close to you makes me wet, Master.” Easing her knees wider apart, she made herself more accessible to him and his lovely, long fingers.

Suddenly, he thrust into her. “Not this time, my sweet.” He jammed his fingers in deep and stirred them around. Before she could react, or beg for more, he pulled them free. “This time, I want you to punish me.”

Stunned by his quick withdrawal, and even more by his words, she gaped at him. “Master?” She wasn’t sure she’d heard him right.

“I want to know how it feels.” He rose to his feet and while she knelt dumbfounded, began stripping out of his clothes. “I see how excited you get. I watch you sink into submission and then explode with the most amazing orgasms. I want to experience it, too, if I can."

Jade wondered if he was serious or trying to trap her in some weird way. *Will he really let me show him? He must know this is a dream of mine. Could it be his too?*

His shirt hit the floor, and a moment later his pants landed on top of it. His socks and underpants were last on the pile. He stood in front of her, his prick swollen, but not hard, nestled in its thatch of wiry black pubic hair.

"Jade, I want you to show me how to submit." He dropped to his knees in front of her, spreading them to about the width of his shoulders, just like he'd taught her to do. Straightening his back, he thrust his chest out and lowered his eyes so he was looking at a spot on the floor in front of her. "I want to learn what it feels like, and I don't trust anyone to do it but you." He hesitated a moment, before adding, "Please."

She could refuse. Tell him, "No, I can't." He'd understand; she was sure of it. But he might never ask again. Just the thought of taking him into that excruciating, wonderful place, excited her beyond anything she'd ever imagined. Taking a deep breath, she knew she had to try. The soft humming of her sex added to her certainty.

Her heart drummed wildly against her ribs, threatening to burst. She rose to her feet, and even though her knees trembled, she went to the chair by the door and slowly dressed: bikini panties, because he liked them, a half-cup bra, again because he liked it, and a pale blue slip dress, because he said the color went so well with her light complexion and blonde hair. *All for him,* she thought and smiled.

Barefoot, she approached and stopped a foot from him. She bent and ran her hand across his shoulder and down his back. "You have to know, this is a fantasy I've had for years. This makes me wet. You make me wet," she murmured, feeling a thrill at the new name she had for him. "Do you know what you're asking, boy?"

He stiffened under her hand. Whether it was the name or the question she didn't know, and at that moment she didn't much care. The transition from submissive to dominant took but a moment, albeit with a little uncertainty.

"Yes, I think so," he replied just as softly.

"Bend forward. Head to the floor. Hands behind your neck." She barked the instructions out, wanting him to really understand what he was getting himself into—wanting to push herself out of the role she usually played. *If he's going to balk, now's the time to find out.*

He hesitated, just an instant, as if he had to make a decision. He sighed. Bending forward, he placed his hands behind his head, fingers laced. A moment later, he was in the position she requested.

He wriggled, and that made her smile. She was sure he'd never actually been in that position before. If he'd spread his legs a little more before bending forward, it would have been easier. Of course, his ass would have been on much better display then too. He wasn't ready for that, yet.

"If I'd responded as you just did, what would you have done?" She ran a hand over his lower back then his bottom. His skin was warm, more so than usual.

"I would have warmed your butt, Ma'am," he replied, grudgingly.

"You don't sound too pleased." A smile tugged at her mouth. She wondered if he'd ever been spanked. "Did you expect me to simply turn you over my knee and spank you?"

"I'm not sure. I didn't think too much about how you'd go about doing it, I guess, Ma'am." He shifted again, his knees sliding over the carpet, spreading wider, and winced from the rug burn.

She ran the tips of her fingers along the inside of his thigh, from the crook of his knee to just below his dangling balls. Skipping across, she trailed down the other thigh, from groin to knee. His sac tightened, the skin crinkling. His cock thickened. He was nearly erect.

"Comfy?" She traced her fingers up again, enjoying the feel of him trembling. She didn't detour this time, but caressed him boldly, exploring the weight and girth of him. Using her free hand, she stroked each of his cheeks, priming him for what was to come.

"Yes, kind of, thank you, Ma'am."

Raising the hand high above his ass, she held it up for a long drawn-out moment, waiting while he squirmed a little more before bringing it down with a resounding smack squarely in the middle of his right buttock.

He yelped and jerked forward, his bottom clenched tight. "Ouch! Hey, what—"

The next slap landed just as sharply on his other cheek, cutting off whatever he'd been about to say. Twice more she struck, and twice more he yelped and jerked forward. He did, however, manage to keep his fingers laced behind his neck.

Returning her hand to his behind, she caressed the faint red handprints, admiring the growing heat, the smooth taut flesh. "You should never lie, and you should never argue or complain unless you're in some distress. You know better, don't you, boy?"

He stiffened. It took him a moment, and she was sure he'd bit his lip to keep from snapping a reply. "Yes, Ma'am, I know better. I'm sorry."

"Are you comfortable?"

Instantly, he replied, "No, Ma'am. My knees are sore."

"Thank you," she replied levelly. "I'll keep that in mind." Slipping her fingers along the deep cleft separating his buttocks, she twirled the index finger around the dark, swirled pucker. Gentle pressure allowed her finger entrance; a fluttering grasp tickled the digit. Pulling free, she continued her journey downward to the bulge below. Lingering, she stroked and massaged the bump, but his testicles shifted, drawing her attention.

Instead of taking them into her hand again, she trailed a finger around them, nudging them with her knuckles, twirling her finger into the longer hair along his inner thigh. They shifted, pulling up closer to his body, as if in search of attention.

"Do you like it when I touch you?" It was difficult to keep her voice even and her hand from trembling, but she did her best, determined to do this right.

"Yes, of course I do," Brian snapped, his irritation showing. "This isn't what I was expecting, though."

"Ah, I see," she murmured, continuing to trace small circles around his genitals. His shaft lengthened, close to reaching its fully erect state. "But, it's not up to you, is it?"

Again, there was a pause before he answered. "No, it's not. It's completely up to you, isn't it?"

Jade chuckled and replied, "Yes, completely." She wondered if he understood, really understood, what that meant and what was happening to him. "You expected me to what? Just spank you, tie you to the bench and beat your ass?"

"Yes, I suppose that's exactly what I thought."

Slipping her hand under him, she took firm hold of his shaft, as close to the base as she could. She didn't masturbate him. Instead, she tightened her fist and felt the pulse. It thickened even more. She waited breathlessly for his shaft to swing upward and tap against his belly, the fingers of her other hand continuing their tormenting dance around his balls. Once satisfied he was fully erect, she said, "This is turning you on. Why?" She moved her fist along his erection, milking him in a slow deliberate pull.

"Yes," he replied, his voice gruff with excitement. "It's turning me on. I don't know why."

She released him and moved beside him. "But, you must know what you find exciting. Tell me." Poised, knowing the answer eluded him. It must.

He shifted, his head rising off the floor.

Jade was expecting it, and quickly put her hands on his shoulders, pushing him back down. "Stay put, boy. I asked you a question," she snarled. Under her hand, the muscles in his shoulders writhed.

"Bitch," he whispered.

Chuckling, Jade knew she was on the right track. "Slide your hands between your legs, reach back and grab your ankles." She barked her commands, wanting to shock him into complying quickly, without thinking.

It worked. In the time it took her to straighten up, and get the Ping-Pong paddle he often used from the cabinet, he was in position, his buttocks spread, giving her a lovely view of parted cheeks and the tackle below.

"What did you call me?" She didn't touch him, but stood back admiring the sight, gauging his discomfort, and his excitement.

He shifted his legs. Adjusting his hands, he tried to draw his knees closer together, but couldn't. "Bitch, Ma'am."

"Yes, I thought I heard that." The paddle felt large in her hand, exciting. "Are you horny?" Her hand was sweaty, the wooden handle slippery. She tightened her grip.

After a thoughtful moment of silence, he replied, "Yes, very horny."

"Don't release your ankles."

He turned his head, eyes catching her just as she swung the paddle sharply down, connecting with his right asscheek. "You will not show disrespect for me."

The taut skin of his knuckles flashed white against the darker flesh of his hand and ankle as his grip tightened. His head shot back, and his mouth opened in a silent cry of surprise.

Another swat, equally hard, slammed down on his left cheek. "You will answer questions when asked."

Again, his head jerked back, and this time a stifled grunt reached her ears.

"Punishment will be meted out as I wish, not to your expectations." Another blow struck, landing on the lower half of his asscheek. The next followed a heartbeat later, not giving him time to catch his breath.

"I will now punish you. I'll stop when I think it's time to stop."

She paced herself, knowing from experience to wait until Brian exhaled before landing a blow. Watching him breathe and shift, the tensing of muscles along his back and shoulders, and the way his erection swung between his widespread thighs, excited her enormously.

Her lust burned brightly, growing, engulfing her as the color of his ass deepened from pink to red, then crimson. Her cunt clenched with each blow. When the round paddle struck, her breath caught. Her nipples grew taut, ached to have clamps or fingers pinching them.

Her right arm grew tired, so she shifted to his other side and swung backhand. The blows weren't as powerful, and she knew he'd be grateful for that. His bottom literally radiated heat. The nerve endings would be screaming.

"Please," he gasped, finally, suddenly. He turned to face her again, tears brightening his eyes.

She lowered her arm and knelt behind him, dropping the paddle to the floor. "Put your head down," she said, firmly.

"Yes, Ma'am," he gulped. His forehead returned to the floor.

Reaching for him, she caressed his sore behind, working the pain in and soothing him. Bending forward, she pressed her cheek against his ass and sighed at its heat. "Now just feel." Her hands moved from his bottom to his genitals. She wasn't surprised to find him still swollen but not fully erect. It only took a stroke to bring him back, and another few had him gasping. Easing the skin up and down his shaft added to her excitement as well. In no time, she found herself wanting to forget the play—to bend and take him in her mouth.

Determined to carry the game through, she smiled. It wasn't just Brian who was learning something new.

She toyed with him, pinching the head of his prick each time he came close to orgasm. His moans of pleasure guided her; his groans of frustration amused her. When he thrust his hips back and forth, she slapped his bottom, reminding him of who was in control. His yelp of pain made her shudder.

A moment later, he thrust again, and she slapped his ass. After the fifth swat, she released him and picked up the paddle. As she looked down at him, he appeared and sounded like he'd run a marathon, gasping, shuddering, his muscles clenching spasmodically.

"Do you want something?" she asked, breathing heavily herself.

"Yes. Please, Ma'am. I want to come."

"Do you want me to use the paddle?"

"I don't know. Dear god, Jade, what are you doing to me?"

He peered over his shoulder at her, and she saw his lust, his need to come, and smiled down at him. "I've done what you asked. I punished you."

"Yes, but..."

"Never mind *but*. I asked you a question." Her voice was firm, surprisingly so.

"Yes," he said. His voice was barely loud enough to reach her. But, he'd said it and that was all she needed.

"You may come," she said, reaching for the paddle and lifting it high. Bringing it down, she softened the blow, and took hold of his shaft at the same time. Stroking him, stimulating the nerve endings she'd already prepared for the pleasure she hoped to give him, she masturbated him. Her fingers wandered everywhere, from the tip of his erection to the puckered opening to his anus. The paddle dropped; she used her hand—a much better tool at this stage.

"Yes," he growled, lunging ahead. His thighs tensed, and a stream of white shot across the floor beneath him. The next stroke sent another ribbon of come after the first. The rest oozed over her hand, drooling to the floor, testament to his pleasure. He shuddered, and thrust again, and again, while she held his prick snugly. His orgasm seemed to go on for minutes rather than seconds. Finally, his muscles lost their tenseness and he simply crouched and swayed. A moment later, he collapsed onto his belly, breathless, gasping.

The handle of the paddle being rubbed between the slick folds of her panty-clad cunt was all it took. Her clit pulsed and her juices flowed freely along the wooden shaft. She cried out, her hand suddenly drenched as she too climaxed. The vision of him, body tensed, the red welts on his ass hot against her palm, sent another harsh shudder through her. Soaring, gliding between geysers of heat roaring through her veins, Jade wallowed in the waves of bliss. The power of control was more than she'd expected—more than she'd ever dared dream. Yet, when the gut-wrenching climax ended she longed for the aftercare of her master. The tender stroking and caresses he lavished her with.

I am a true slut, she mused and smiled. Dropping the paddle to the floor, Jade lay beside him, her master, and gently caressed his face. "I love you, Master. Are you all right?"

"Yes." He peered into her eyes. "It's so intense. My god, is that what it's always like for you? I felt like my insides were coming out. And, my ass is on fire."

Smiling, she replied, "Yes, Master, always. Would you like me to get the cream?"

He thought for a moment, and she saw the power in him. "No, I want to experience this, for a while." He pulled her into his arms, his face buried in her hair. "I love you, Jade."

Snuggling in, her heart close to exploding with love, she replied, "I love you too, Brian, my husband, my master. You've given me such an enormous gift this evening. Thank you."

"Time for bed, sweetheart. I want to make love to you. If I can."

Chuckling, Jade stroked his thigh and saw his cock twitch. "I'm sure we'll manage."

DO YOU SEE WHAT I FEEL?

Teresa Noelle Roberts

I took a deep breath and felt the silky constriction, both comforting and arousing, of the ropes—chest harness, corset, and teasing crotch binding—I wore under my red turtleneck sweater dress. Erik had suggested the dress for its relative innocence; it was calf length and it skimmed my body loosely enough that you'd have to look twice to make out I wore something unusual underneath. Erik had made sure the ropes weren't screamingly obvious, just as he'd made sure the shibari was neat and elegant, and that the crotch ropes were tight enough to tantalize me, but not enough to either irritate that most sensitive skin or let me get off before he was good and ready. (Dammit.)

I'd laughed about his precision with the ropes, and the way he chose the outfit so carefully to suggest and yet conceal them. "Ryo's blind, right? That's the point of this game. So what does it matter?"

Erik said, "Ryo's definitely blind. As for the point of this game..." He gave me one of those secretive, naughty smiles of his, the kind that reaches out and tickles my clit. "Other than turning us both on? You'll figure it out soon enough."

Then he grabbed a strategic knot through the soft knit of the dress and twisted.

The ropes tugged at my labia, pulling them open.

My husband is evil and perverted and I love him for it.

God, I was wet already, slicker than I'd realized. Slick with the caress of ropes and with the knowledge that I was going to be shown off, albeit to someone who might not be aware of it.

I'd probably end up naked save for ropes at some point, naked in front of someone who'd just go on talking with me like nothing was different because he wouldn't know anything was, wouldn't know I was bare and bound and by that point most likely dripping in front of him, trying to carry on a conversation while aching for him to leave so Erik could spank me or fuck me or whatever he had in mind as a final round to the game. Erik's games were always worthwhile in the end.

And always came with an unexpected twist.

I should have known that whatever assumptions I'd made were slightly off.

For instance, I'd imagined Ryo as one of those quietly brilliant Asian American science majors who was now grown up and making big biotech bucks but was still slightly geeky. Probably because, except for the Asian American part, that's what Erik's like. He may be wonderfully kinky, but what can I say? When he's not tying me up and having his wicked way with me, he plays Dungeons and Dragons with a gaggle of other thirty-something geniuses with similar cases of arrested development. (Including me. Yeah, we have more than a few things in common besides hot sex.)

But the man who came to our door, guided by a golden

retriever so well-groomed she practically gleamed...if he'd been in a Japanese movie, he'd have been evil, doomed to a tragic death, or possibly both, because the beautiful men always are. He had sleek, shoulder-length blue-black hair; a body to die for, not much taller than I am, but perfectly proportioned; golden skin, killer cheekbones, and a smile that would have melted my panties if I'd been wearing any. He was dressed all in shades of gray, from his topcoat to his shoes, and just a little too well for a dinner at a friend's house; I guessed the monotone might be less a fashion statement than a practicality for someone who couldn't see, but it looked yummy.

There were a few formalities—introductions, taking Ryo's coat, Ryo taking his guide dog out of harness. (The dog promptly fell asleep—I guess getting Ryo out here on the commuter rail from Boston was quite an adventure.) When that was settled, but before we sat down, I repeated, "Hi, I'm Carla," and hesitantly extended my hand. I was surprised by how readily Ryo followed my voice and clasped it.

And even more surprised when he said, "May I? I like to see who I'm talking to." I caught Erik's eye, saw him nod, and muttered, "Yes." Ryo's strong arms drew me in.

He ran his hands up my arms to my shoulders.

Paused where the ropes crossed over, giving a slight grin and nod.

Ran his hands through my hair and down my back, swiftly and lightly, but there was no way he could have missed the ropes under the soft knit.

Or, I suspected, the way I was trembling.

Finally, he raised his hands to my face. Gentle fingertips explored my features: traced my eyelids, feathered over my eyebrows, highlighted the shape of my cheekbones, got to know my nose, cupped my cheeks, outlined my chin.

It was one of the most incredibly intimate things anyone had ever done to me (and believe me, Erik has done a lot of incredibly intimate things to me, including some that are illegal in several Southern states and the District of Columbia).

The ropes seemed tighter, as if my entire body had grown more sensitive, as if my breasts and pussy had swollen from Ryo's touch on my face.

I closed my eyes and surrendered to the sensation, fighting not to moan. It was just Ryo's way of seeing, right?

Ryo chuckled deep in his throat. "Erik, you dog," he said. "You didn't tell me Carla's beautiful."

"Liar. I told you..."

"You told me she was hot, and I agree. But she's also beautiful. Some women are one and not the other, but she's both. And I bet she has a very sensual mouth."

I froze. As he traced the shape of my lips, I struggled not to kiss that sure finger, to lick at it.

It was all too easy to imagine it circling my nipple with the same delicate precision, or—oh, my god, on my clit.

I couldn't help it. I moaned.

Ryo slipped his finger between my parted lips.

My instincts had all sorts of ideas, but I am married, even if ours is a slightly unusual marriage. I opened my eyes, looked toward Erik as best I could.

He smiled and nodded. Yes. All part of the game, or at least something he was comfortable to make part of the game.

License to play!

I intended to suck that finger like it was a mini-cock, to give Ryo back some of his own teasing medicine.

Instead, his finger caressed my tongue, sending shivers through my body and straight to my already aching pussy. I sucked, and he caressed, and I leaned into Ryo's body, just a bit, and felt delicious hardness adjusting the lines of his elegant charcoal pants.

Ryo slipped his finger from my mouth, pulled me closer, ran both hands down my back again. This time, they weren't light, but firm and bold, exploring. And this time, he didn't stop politely at the small of my back, but followed the ropes down, feeling how they dipped between my buttocks. He chuckled again, approvingly, and gave the ropes a little tug.

My lips swelled under the caress of the ropes, and my head swam.

This wasn't what I expected. He wasn't what I expected.

But he was making me melt, and it wasn't just a handsome man's hands on me, although I wasn't about to complain about that. I'm more than a little bit of an exhibitionist, and this wasn't the first time Erik had found a way to show me off to an appreciative audience, but the way Ryo was seeing me with his hands was something new. It was far more intimate than simply being watched, and yet curiously impersonal in some ways. I got the feeling he'd explore anything new and interesting with as much delicacy and curiosity.

Although probably without a tempting hard-on.

Erik stood there watching (and probably getting hard himself) as his friend and I drove each other crazy.

And then, when my body was turning to liquid fire and Ryo bent his head down as if he was thinking about kissing me, Erik—damn him and his games!—said something studiedly innocuous about predinner drinks.

I'm not sure how to describe the noise I made. I'm afraid whining was involved as well as some more appealing elements like moaning.

Ryo laughed and said, "I'd love a scotch." He gave my butt a light squeeze before pulling away. "Carla, would you help me find a seat?"

He took my arm innocently, as if he hadn't just been driving me wild—then touched the bare skin of my wrist so lightly and yet so deliciously that I shivered.

I was so going to get Erik for not warning me that his blind friend wasn't going to be an innocent pawn in our game, that he was apparently just as toppy and arousingly evil as Erik.

On the other hand, would it have been nearly as much fun if I'd known?

Cocktails and dinner passed with excruciating slowness. I barely tasted my wine, although I might have sipped more of it than I meant to, couldn't be sure what I was eating even though I'd helped cook it. The guys kept up a stream of light, suggestive banter the whole time that kept me distracted, focused on the ropes and the throbbing, aching territory between my thighs rather than on food. That the banter was about me, but between them, just made it worse, or maybe better. It was especially unnerving—and exciting—that while Erik kept smiling at me, touching my hand, including me in little ways, Ryo didn't even glance in my direction. The part of my brain that was still working logically realized that, blind since birth, he didn't bother pretending he could see who he was talking to.

The part of my brain that was playing in the gutter, and that was most of it, relished feeling like an object—a beautiful, fascinating object, sure, but an object—for the guys' amusement. Sometimes in our games I showed myself off, and felt powerful, but this time I was being shown off and that was hot too: wrapped up like a present and tied with a bow, like a special present I was being shown off to Erik's friend.

Or offered to him.

How far would it go? We'd never involved others in our games beyond watching and being watched and some mild teasing caresses, but we were both open to the idea under the right circumstances.

Even though I'd just met Ryo, my body thought this was the right circumstances. My mind? Well, I trust my husband, and he'd known this guy since they were undergraduates.

And even if that wasn't what Erik had in mind, I knew we weren't done. The conversation had layers, and I had a feeling that the guys had something planned, something they were talking around just enough to make me crazy with curiosity and lust.

After we ate, I offered to make coffee. Not that I wanted coffee—I wanted Erik, or Ryo, or ideally, both of them—but I figured if I stepped out of the room, they could finish their plotting without having to be all cryptic.

As soon as I stood, though, Erik said, "No. Stay here. Ryo, would you like to check my work? It's been a long time."

"Hate to think you'd forgotten anything." He turned his face to where he figured I was—I was unnerved by how close he got, when he'd been talking around me for so long. "Carla," he said with exaggerated politeness, "would you take off your dress, please?"

His voice was almost as caressing as his hands had been and I had to grab a chair because my knees went wobbly. Trembling, I reached for the hem of my dress, but "No, let me help you," Erik said. He crouched down, grabbed the hem, and lifted it.

I expected him to go slowly, to tease me further even if Ryo couldn't appreciate it, but instead he had it to my shoulders in a flash. I raised my arms over my head so he could pull it off.

He did. And then he grabbed my wrists and lifted me up until my tiptoes just brushed the floor. Erik is about six five, with big, powerful hands (he works on it just so he can pull off tricks like this) so it was like suspension bondage without the suspension, a lovely strain that pulled the ropes tighter against my oversensitive lips, arched my breasts forward, and made me even more aware of being helplessly, deliciously on display.

"She's ready for you, Ryo," he said. "Come see what I've done."

And of course, there was only one way for him to see.

With his hands.

He started at the top, caressed my face again, followed the lines of my throat to my collarbone, and followed that line to the ropes.

He traced those down to where they started wrapping my chest; three wrappings of rope there, and he followed all of them across my body, checked where they went between my breasts. His fingers barely grazed the sensitive valley, concentrating instead on the ropes, but that was enough to make me squirm and moan. He reached the band of ropes underneath, traced those as well. This time his touch, by accident or design, was less precise, stroking the plump bottom curve of my breasts. He was nowhere near the nipple, but that flesh was almost as sensitive now as my nipples normally were. I bit my lip, but the "Oh, god" was still audible.

Ryo chuckled, and the appreciation in the chuckle was like another caress. He liked my reactions, and I liked that he liked them.

Liked it enough that moisture was trickling down my legs.

Ryo's hands moved lower, to the ropes corseting my waist. "You changed ropes here," he said, stroking one area repeatedly. He wasn't touching skin, except through rope, but it still set the skin there on fire and sent the flames traveling to my clit.

"Yeah. I'm surprised you can tell. They're the same kind of rope."

"Close, but not quite. I'd like to see how you handled the

transition. It felt pretty smooth through her dress."

Erik turned me around like the thing I felt myself to be.

Ryo examined the knot work where the two ropes joined. "Very neat. A lot of people don't bother to make the back so tidy."

"You taught me well."

When I could string two coherent sentences together, I was going to ask for that story. A good story is the next best thing to being there, and since I couldn't go back in time and watch Ryo teaching Erik, I'd like to hear all the juicy details. But for now I could only relax and enjoy the sensations as Ryo examined all the knots and transitions on my back. It took a long time, and before he was done, Erik was letting me lean on him because I was shaking so much.

Or maybe it was just because he wanted me there. He kept kissing me, sending me soaring even higher. His sweater and jeans felt wonderfully rough against my bare skin and the wool of his sweater was almost painful, but in a good way, on my nipples. He pressed his crotch against my thigh and ground, and I could feel how hard he was, how much he was enjoying the show and the act of showing me off. I kept trying to move so he'd rub it between my legs, but he was having none of that. He wanted to keep the long tease going, and maybe—at least I liked to think so—he might have found that a little too much himself.

Finally Ryo said, his voice husky, "Great work, Erik. At least as good as mine. Turn her around. There's one last thing I want to check."

Erik whispered in my ear, "Are you ready?"

I had a pretty good idea of what was coming, and all I could possibly say was "God, yes. Please!"

Erik neatly turned me around and lifted me up again, using only one hand, arching me back against his body. He reached around me with the other, simultaneously hugging me close and pinching my nipple. I clenched and nearly came.

I was perversely glad I didn't quite make it, though. Ryo had something in mind and I was waiting for that.

Ryo put his hands on my waist.

Ran them down over the rope-covered curve of my belly.

Found where the ends of the crotch ropes were neatly woven into the waist wrap.

Then, excruciatingly slowly, Ryo traced the two ropes down, following them to where they were holding my pussy lips open.

"So wet," he said. "So very wet. You'll have to wash the rope." As he spoke, he stroked the damp, slippery rope, barely touching my flesh, not touching my clit at all. I needed to come so badly it hurt, but even the ache felt good.

I cocked my hips toward him, said, "Please. Please. Oh, god, please," or at least something like that.

"One last thing to check," Ryo said, and flicked my clit.

The guide dog started awake as I screamed and then screamed some more. His touch was as sure and delicate there as it had been everywhere else, but at this point he could have been clumsy as a teenage boy still trying to figure out female anatomy and I'd have gone off like a rocket.

"And that's the final test," he said, clearly talking to Erik, not to me. "The prettiest rope work in the world is useless unless the result's a wet, screaming woman."

Erik eased me down and I slumped between the two men, feeling like I'd just run a very special kind of marathon.

Only then did Ryo kiss me.

He kissed as deliciously as he did everything else, but when his watch quietly intoned the hour, he pulled away. "I should get going," he said. "If I catch the next train, I'll get home about when Jessie does—and the deal was I could come play without her today as long as I saved most of my energy for home. She was so pissed she got called into work today, but she's too new at the job to get away with saying no."

"Bring her next time," I said, surprised at my boldness coming back so quickly, surprised, in fact, that I could talk again. "That is…there'll be a next time?"

"I hope so," both men said at once.

"Jessie likes to show off about as much as you do," Ryo said, "and she likes to watch too."

"And you have to show me that tortoiseshell pattern again," Erik said. "I thought I remembered it, but I don't think it's right."

"Be glad to, my friend," Ryo said, and called for his dog. "If the ladies are up for it, I'll show you on Carla and let you practice on Jessie. That way Carla can see what you're doing. Never know when an extra pair of hands could be useful. Does that sound good?"

I managed to stammer out "Yes," but it wasn't easy, because my mind was already flooding with images of Ryo tying me up while Erik and Jessie watched, Erik tying Jessie up while I watched, and Ryo "supervising" in his own special way that was sure to drive both Jessie and me crazy.

Fortunately Erik was thinking more clearly than I and managed to see Ryo off safely. He offered a ride to the train, but Ryo laughed and said, "It's not like walking in the dark bothers me, man, and I think you have something to do."

Which he did, bending me over the arm of the couch as soon as Ryo left and driving his cock deep inside me.

It wasn't until we were boneless, sated, and curled up on the couch together that I managed to ask something that had been plaguing me. "How did the blind guy master rope bondage anyway?"

"How he learned is a long story and you'd better ask him. As to how he does it, how do you think? By touch...and very, very slowly."

And just thinking about that was enough to get us started on the next round.

BETTER BENT THAN BROKEN

Amanda Fox

The video wasn't something I was supposed to see. I found it by accident and I'll admit, at the time, the images of all those men sucking each other off and penetrating each other in rows and stacks of bodies came as a complete shock. It wasn't like anything I'd ever seen before, and the weirdest part about it was the fact that I'd actually found it on my husband's computer.

"Ummm, John. Can I ask you something?" The moment occurred precisely one week after John's return from a month-long business trip in Dubai.

"Sure, sweetheart. What is it?" He was reading the newspaper.

"Well, this morning my computer wasn't working, so I used your laptop to pay some bills and I sort of—I mean, I wasn't snooping or anything—but I found something."

"What's that, love?" he asked innocently.

"Ummm well, I found some porn."

"Oh, you naughty girl. Did it make you want to touch yourself?" Admittedly, watching dirty movies was something we did on a regular basis.

"Not exactly." I paused, the hitch in my voice causing him to look up.

"What's wrong?"

"Well, it was a movie about men—a whole bunch of men—and not just that, but there were quite a few movies. Like a lot. Like hundreds."

"Oh," he said, suddenly nervous.

"John. I'm not sure what to think. They are yours, right? It is your computer."

"I didn't figure that you'd ever see them. Not that I was hiding them from you but..." he stammered. "Well, I just didn't... I mean it was... Oh, god, never mind." He shook his head and stared at the floor.

"I don't know what to say," I sighed, both of us hanging in silence. After two very long minutes, John held out his hand. "Come here, Karen. I can explain."

I couldn't move. "Go ahead," I said, tapping my foot.

"Okay, I haven't told you because I wasn't sure how you'd react. Anyway, it has nothing to do with our relationship. So I like watching men have sex. Big deal. It doesn't matter. I still love you the same now as I did fifteen years ago and you're still the sexiest person on earth to me."

I could feel my face getting warmer. "I just don't get it, John. How can watching men fuck do anything for you? You're not gay are you?" My heart skipped a beat. "Or are you?"

"No, I'm not gay. I simply saw a movie once when I was searching the Internet and I kind of liked it. Since then I've found myself going back for more." His confession was coming more easily now. "At first, I tried to ignore how it made me feel, but over the years I've decided that life is too short to beat myself up over it."

"Okay, but how can you like to watch men and still want to

have sex with me?" My eyes were burning.

"Don't cry, Karen," he soothed, crossing the room. "Sex with you has always been amazing and very satisfying." Gathering me in close, he seductively pressed his groin into my belly.

"You wouldn't lie to me, I hope," I sniffed.

'Never." John hugged me tight. "You should know that by now."

"So, does that mean you want to have sex with me and with men?"

"Well, I don't know that I could have a relationship with a man—not like with you—but I will say that I think touching is touching. If you are attracted to someone, why should gender matter? Of course, you have to be open to that kind of thing."

"And are you telling me that you are 'open' to that kind of thing?"

"Karen..."

"Well, are you?"

"I'm not sure."

"John, I don't think I could handle you sleeping with anyone else." The room was beginning to spin.

"Karen, you don't have to worry. We're married, remember?" He smiled. "I don't ever recall us making extramarital affairs part of the deal."

"But there were so many movies, John. So many. That must mean something." And for me, it did mean something—something that I needed to work out whether John thought so or not.

"Stand up and take off your pants," I declared, waiting for John to expose his muscular, cocoa brown cheeks.

"Are you sure you're ready for this?"

"Positive."

"You don't have to do it, you know."

"Life is about change, John. You said so yourself. We must all grow, right? So this is something I have to do—something we have to do. It seems to be a rather important part of your sexuality, wouldn't you agree?"

"I told you, Karen, it's just a fantasy."

"Come on, John, be real. Your little movie collection makes this more like an obsession. It must be something that you at least want to try." Anger and jealousy over this issue still had my blood boiling.

"Believe whatever you want, but I'm telling you that I would be just fine exploring this interest all on my own. It doesn't have to be with other people. Not even you." Despite his words however, John was eagerly unbuttoning his jeans. Pushing them past his hips, he let his pants fall poignantly to the floor.

In that moment, I wanted to be open with John—to understand his needs and desires—but I also wanted to smack him hard upside the head. Lucky for him, my compassionate side won out. "John, I want us to be able to share everything and I want you to be happy." I took the strap-on out of its box.

"I'm already happy, Karen," he said, the growing bulge in his boxers further debunking his claim.

"So what's with the heat-seeking missile?" I smirked. "I haven't even touched you yet."

"That's all for you, love." He bent down to slip off his socks.

"Sure, John." Without question, I knew that my life was about to change—at least from my point of view. My man's man, my alpha male, my dictator in the bedroom, my man who once only liked women, my penetrator, my straight-laced husband John, had transformed into someone I did not recognize. "Now I know that we've discussed this, but I've taken a few liberties in preparation for this momentous occasion."

I needed some control over the situation. Not that I wasn't about to be the person in charge, but what I needed was to do something unexpected—something to show John that I wasn't a total prude.

John's eyes bulged out like maybe I'd gone off the deep end. "Oh?" he gulped.

"Here. You have to put on this blindfold first," I said, walking over to fasten a satin scarf around his head. "There. Now it's time for you to get naked."

"Anything you say, Karen," John acquiesced, sliding down his underwear to expose a lofty erection.

"Wow John, you're just an erectile superstar. Why don't you touch it for me? Show me how hard it can get." And like a first-rate student, my brown-skinned Adonis slid his hand up and down the shiny, mahogany shaft, more than happy to oblige. As he played, I reached under the mattress to retrieve his surprise, nonchalantly adding, "That's it. I want you to be rock hard."

"What are you doing?" he asked, his member now the darkest shade of purple I'd ever seen it.

"Be patient," I chided, inserting a DVD into the player, and after a few technical adjustments, the sounds of four men in the throes of passion filled the room. "There. Now tell me, what do you hear?"

"I hear people having sex," he answered plainly.

"Yes, John. Actually, it's a group of men having sex—handsome, muscular men, just like you. And by the looks of it, they are having fun. A lot of fun."

"Really?" John asked inquisitively.

"Yes, really. They are all very, very hard." Moving in, I shoved at his thighs, forcing his legs apart. "Do you like listening to those men fucking, John?"

"I guess so," he groaned faintly.

"What do you mean 'you guess so'? Do you or don't you?" I was trying to be tough.

Milking his cock hard, John attempted to get into the game. "Yes. I do."

"Good, because I want you to listen to them while I lick you. Pretend that they are right here in this room. Pretend that they are right beside you. Pretend that it's not me, but one of them licking your cock."

"Okay," he said, visibly trembling.

When I flicked at him with my tongue and his penis actually jumped, I knew immediately what sort of direction our sex life was about to take. Not quite sure how I felt about the whole situation but committed to behaving unconditionally where my husband was concerned, I began sucking and maneuvering my way up and down his engorged penis. When he began to shudder a few moments later, I immediately moved back. "Onto your hands and knees, John," I snapped, leading him over to the bed.

"Are you going to fuck me now?" he asked tentatively.

"Not yet," I said. "First I want you to show me your ass." Once he'd positioned himself on all fours—the men on the television groaning and grunting like bears in the background—I smoothed over his cheeks with one hand and pulled roughly on his testicles with the other. "You're winking at me, John," I giggled, watching his third eye pucker and release. "Now hold still." I then leaned forward and licked a slow circle around the rim of his tunnel.

"That feels so good," he moaned, arching back at my face.

"I'm glad you like it," I purred, dipping the tip of my tongue inside. "Because I like it too." And it was true. The tang of him, while new to me, was tantalizing and I couldn't help but go at him full force after that, surging and slurping, prying and squeezing until his entire backside was glazed with fluid.

When my thumb accidentally breached his cleft however, John lurched forward. "Jesus, Karen. Stop!"

"What's wrong?" I asked, watching his penis bob up and down above the blankets, his testicles a tight little ball. "I am going to fuck you, aren't I?"

"Yes, but..." It was obvious that he needed a short reprieve.

"Well, we can't have that," I teased. "We're just getting started. Perhaps now would be a good time to take off your blindfold."

"Good idea," he sighed, waiting patiently for me to undo the knot, and once liberated, his focus shot straight to the men fornicating on the screen.

"Do you like that, John? Would you like them to suck your cock?" I asked, roughly taking him back into my mouth.

"Yes. God, yes," he declared, stabbing at my face. In no time, he was threatening to explode once again.

Retreating, I whispered, "You are not allowed to cum yet John, remember?"

At my behest, he gave the base of his penis a good squeeze. "Maybe you should fuck me now." It was almost a plea.

"Yes. I think you're more than ready. But you do need to help me with this." I reached for our new toy.

"Sure," he said, examining the contraption. "See, there's a part for you." He pointed to the shorter of the two dildos. "And a part for me. Now lie down and I'll hook you up."

As ready as I was ever going to be, I spread my legs and like a scientist putting the finishing touches on his newest invention, John worked the smaller of the two plugs slowly around the outside of my vagina. "My goodness, Karen, I don't think I've ever seen you this wet before." And I was wet, my vulva and inner thighs a glistening canvas.

“I think I need to cum, John,” I replied. “My vagina actually hurts.” My pussy was throbbing.

“Did it excite you to lick my ass? Or was it all those men fucking that did it?”

“Please, John. Help me,” I whined, desperate for some relief.

“Oh, so you get to cum but I don’t?’

“Well, I can cum more than once. Can you?” Grinning, I brought my heels in, urging him to deeper penetration.

“I could if you waited long enough,” John laughed and with the moves of a maestro, he probed at me until I almost burst.

“More, John. More,” I cried. “Put in the bigger one.”

“You are a greedy girl, aren’t you? The big cock is supposed to be for me.”

“Just fuck me with it first,” I growled, needing all I could get. And when John filled me at last, I bucked and thrashed with such intensity that the world could’ve ended and I wouldn’t even have noticed.

“I like it when you lick my asshole, Karen,” John whispered. “It makes me want to yank on my dick so hard that I shoot all the way across the room.” With that, I began to shatter.

“That’s a good girl, Karen. Let me see you cum,” John growled, his eyes a vehement gold, his hands and knees bracing me open. When he ground into me—twisting and turning the object like he was drilling for oil—I released my soul, forcibly spewing a warm stream of clear liquid all over the bed. “Wow,” John said, gently removing the cock once I’d finished. “You’ve never done that before.”

“You’d be surprised at what I can do,” I purred proudly, rubbing my pussy. “Now it’s your turn, John. But first I think you should suck this cock. See what a woman’s cum tastes like. You do know how to suck a cock, don’t you, John?”

Like I’d said the magic words, John sprung into action,

holding the fake appendage up to his face. "Ummm, smells good, but I think I'll try the big one," he murmured, pushing the longer of the two cylinders past his lips.

"Oh, you're good at that. Can you take it in more?"

Instantly, he deep-throated the thing, straining and choking until presumably the titillation was just too much to handle. Removing it, he eyed me intently. "Please, Karen. Fuck me. I need you to fuck me."

"You're right. It's time. Now hook me up."

Upon fastening the last buckle of the strap-on, John bounced back onto all fours, his ass aimed directly at my artificial dick. "Start with your fingers," he said, looking back over one shoulder.

"Easy there, tiger. You'll get what you're given," I chided, working him first with one, then two, then three, then four digits—inserting and withdrawing the better part of my hand until his back door was a gaping hole.

"Slowly, Karen. Slowly," he gasped when I finally nudged him with the end of the dildo. "I want to make it last."

"How's that?" I asked, dipping in only a fraction of an inch.

John let out a long, low, guttural moan. "That feels fuckin' unbelievable."

Glad that he was enjoying himself, I began to move the rod gently in and out of his welcoming chamber. "Do you want me to fuck you in any special way?"

After a few thrusts, he said, "Can you pull out really slow so that just the tip is inside and then push it all the way back in?" Initially, I wasn't sure how much he could take, but when he started pushing back at me, I got brave and ground into him with my hips. Fully impaled, he cried, "Stop, Karen. I need to cum in your cunt."

"What?" I asked, confused. "I thought I was supposed to do the fucking."

"Just do it." And as I withdrew, he froze. Once emptied however, his virile determination was apparent and he yanked the straps of the contraption furiously from around my hips and thighs. Two seconds later, the double dildo flew across the room. "Good. Now lie on your back and show me your pussy."

Holding the arches of my feet, he then drove into me like a man possessed, pulling all the way out each time to look down at his rock-solid penis. "Jesus, you feel like heaven," he bawled, intentionally heaving us both as close as possible to the television set. "Watch, Karen. Watch them fuck." I glanced sideways. "Their cocks are so hard. I like to be hard like that." His eyes were aflame, his penis a steel missile. "Now watch the guy with the curly hair. He's going to cum soon. You can see it in his face," John said, pounding away at me, his testicles slapping my bottom.

Also focusing on the actors, I took what he gave and just as the man on the screen erupted all over the buttocks of another, John pumped into me with such force that I thought I was going to split in half, unloading into my womanly hollow a torrent that didn't fully leak out for days. I too succumbed for a second time that evening, though I can't even say that I felt it much. I was too numb already.

After the ruckus had turned to a placid pulse, John stroked his fingers down the front of my chest, pausing at my nipples to give them a loving pinch. "I adore your breasts," he sighed. "I've always adored your breasts."

"I'm glad," I replied, both content and relieved. "I'm sooo glad."

SAFE

Vanessa Vaughn

Mara hung up the phone slowly in the dark, placing it gently back on the bedside table. Her fingers toyed with the long cord, tracing the curling rubber-coated surface with her fingertips, absentmindedly winding it around her hand. She couldn't bring herself to call. She crossed, then recrossed her legs, shifting her weight on the mattress.

Dan was always the one to call her, but tonight there was nothing. No phone call. No word. He must have found the paper she had folded so deliberately in his briefcase that morning, the one printed so neatly with those three simple sentences.

As she thought of them, she felt her muscles tense. She hoped he had read her three instructions for the evening, but she also sensed the anticipation twisting inside her. She could feel it curling deep in her stomach, the small of her back, the arches of her feet. She felt the electricity of it; but what emotion was this exactly? Excitement? Perhaps just fear? Whatever it was, she wanted to feel filled with it.

Her eyes moved slowly over the furniture, taking in the familiar features of their bedroom. The moonlight was dim tonight, but traces still shone through the window. Her vision could find the edges of the large dresser and the shining silver mirror above it. She could sense the heavy wooden bed frame that surrounded her. The closet stood open. She could just make out the rows of clothes neatly hanging inside, and the gray box with a dial glinting in the light below them.

She wondered how much time she had. Tonight, he wouldn't arrive as he always did, dropping his wallet and keys casually into the silver dish by the front door, loosening his tie, smelling of clean comfortable cologne as he sorted through the mail. No, she was sure of that. Tonight he would be someone different. Mara thought about what she had written. It was clear. It was simple. She hoped he understood.

She settled in under the heavy comforter. Although she was dressed as she always was for bed, wearing a pink tank top and thin cotton panties, tonight she felt almost naked as she lay there. She felt vulnerable and enticing. The wetness between her legs increased as she tossed and turned in the dark. She stretched, feeling the cool cotton sheets against her bare arms and legs. Slowly, she traced the outline of her body with the edge of her fingernail, feeling the sensation on her skin. Looking down at her pink nipples, she squeezed them gently, watching them harden in the cold air. She thought of Dan, of the sculpted muscles of his wide shoulders, of his large hands and how they would feel holding her down. She shuddered. The waiting made her feel suffocated. She lay with her mouth slightly open and eyes shut, her chest rising and falling in slow measured breaths.

No one would understand. Perhaps he wouldn't understand. Role-playing was supposed to be about dressing as secretaries or nurses or schoolgirls, but that felt so artificial. Alone in the dark,

Mara gently bit her lip. She wasn't a toy to be dressed up and played with. She wanted something more intense.

Her whole body craved it. She craved him, wondering if he could be as aggressive as she wanted him to be. Silently, she wondered if he would be able to play the role she had given him. But she didn't want to be played with, exactly. She wanted to be owned. She remembered the second of the three neatly printed sentences she had written: *Make it rape.*

She rolled onto her stomach with a sigh, trying to relax before he arrived. The ceiling fan turned slowly and rhythmically above her, blowing patterns of cool air across her shoulders. She felt the perfect roundness of her ass in the white cotton, and tried to imagine what it would look like to him. Without thinking, she arched her lower back a little, as if he was watching her, curling the ends of her toes together. Her eyes closed sleepily as she focused on the relaxing heartbeat of the fan, willing her body to relax and wait.

Her eyes fluttered open as she slowly became aware of the sound in the other room. Her limbs felt heavier, her mouth dry. Had she fallen asleep?

Then she heard it again: a muffled squeaking noise, this time followed by a dull thud. For a moment, she forgot where she was. She forgot what exactly she had asked for. In that moment, she only lay there in the large bed, completely relaxed.

But as she allowed herself to notice the noise, it suddenly registered in her head. It was the squeaky sound of a window being pushed open.

Of course! He was coming in through the window in the next room. Immediately, she thought of the first of the three instructions she had written for him that morning: *Tonight, you will be a thief.*

She sat up in bed, now fully awake. Dan was playing the role of a thief. And he was coming in through the window. But what had that thudding sound been? She began to scramble out of bed. As she realized that the thud must have been the sound of him already jumping inside, she saw the bedroom door open with a sudden powerful motion.

She froze.

He seemed huge standing in the small doorway. In the darkness, she could see only his outline. The very dim glow from the other window illuminated the strong line of his shoulders and chest, but his face and most of his body was hidden in shadow.

They both stood still for a moment, gauging each other's reaction. As Mara stared at his clothes in the darkness, trying to see him more clearly, she was suddenly, perfectly aware of her own nakedness. She tugged at the bottom hem of her tank top, pulling it down a bit in an automatic gesture of modesty.

In that moment, she could feel his eyes on her, feel them crawling over her bare legs, her arms, the look of innocent surprise on her face. She wanted him so badly, but wondered if he would go through with this game. Something about his stance in the doorway made her sure that he would.

Mara was suddenly afraid. She imagined the desire that had been building inside him all day. She could sense an air of danger and an exciting menace about his presence. Yes, she was sure he was ready to fuck her.

She decided to play along, but she couldn't believe this was really happening. Just awakening from her sleepy haze, this seemed like part of a dream to her. This couldn't be her. It couldn't be him. She gasped and made a move to crawl across the bed to the far side. But before she could make it across, she felt his hand gripping her ankle.

In one motion, he had crossed from the door to the bed and taken hold of her. He tugged on her leg and pulled her solidly toward him as she twisted her body around. Yes, this was real. Mara let out a noise of frustration and fear as he dragged her close. She was lying on her back now, half on and half off the bed, her legs dangling off the side. He stood in front of her.

She marveled at his strength as he did this. He was a full head taller than her, strong and athletic, but he had never handled her like this before. Roughly, before she knew what was happening, he ripped the pink top off of her and tossed it to the floor.

Yes, she thought. *I want you to use me completely.* She wanted to see how strong his desire for her could be. She wanted him to let go and even scare himself a little. She wanted him to truly take her by force.

He was ready for her. She could feel his cock hard and eager, straining against his pants. The rough fabric brushed against her through her thin panties. Unconsciously, she moved against him, wondering if he could tell how much she wanted it too.

Firmly, before she could speak, he grabbed her by the hips and spun her around. He held her by the back of the neck with one hand, pushing her face into the comforter. She could hear him unzipping his fly behind her as she pretended to resist, twisting to get free. She truly tried to escape. She used all her strength to try to pull herself forward on the bed. She tried to pry his fingers from her neck, but it was no use. He was too strong for her. There was something comforting in the fact that he could dominate her completely. Something safe.

Then she felt it: the smoothness of his skin against hers as he tugged her panties down. She braced herself for him, but it wasn't enough. This was all happening so fast.

He pushed into her violently. She hadn't been completely ready for it. She felt herself tense. Every muscle clenched. Her breath stopped in her throat, as if that first thrust into her held her whole body in check.

For a moment, she felt panic. What if this wasn't Dan at all? She hadn't seen his face. He hadn't even spoken. There was pain in this. It was all so unlike him. But, of course, this was what she had asked for. She felt suddenly guilty and ashamed. It was too much.

He pushed into her again, and she still tensed; but she felt no more panic. Mara could recognize the familiar scent of him. She could hear the familiar timbre in his throat as he grunted with the thrust. Yes, it was him, and he was playing his part completely.

With his free hand, he grabbed one of her wrists and twisted it, pinning her arm behind her back. With the other, he continued to hold the back of her neck, pushing her face firmly into the bed so that she could not see him.

She gave herself up to him in that moment, relaxing completely. He began to fuck her harder and faster. She felt filled with him.

Little patterns of light exploded into her vision behind her tightly shut eyes. Irregular patterns of reds and whites swirled in and out of the dark background with each rough rhythmic thrust. Was it the pain? Her eyelids brushing against the comforter?

Offhandedly, she thought of the third sentence she had written: *We will use the same safeword as always. Fractal.*

It was a cold word, mathematical, sensible. Everything that was irrelevant to sex. Or was it really? After all, fractals looked like organic things, not something calculated and numerical. They looked alive, like the swirling patterns behind her eyes. They were repetitive, like the all-consuming motion of him pushing into her again and again. Yes, she could easily say it if she wanted to. She could turn her head to the side and speak the word clearly and this would stop, but for that reason she did not want it to stop.

His grip on her wrist tightened. She could feel his fingers digging into her. She wondered how she looked to him in such a vulnerable position, with her arm twisted behind her, her panties slid down just low enough for him to take her. She arched her back, angling herself a little closer to him as he screwed her.

She took in the completeness of this scenario, the simplicity of it. She was his victim and he would rape her. He would have what he wanted. It was as simple and inevitable as that.

It was impossible to push him away. Struggling would do no good, so she allowed every part of her body to relax, melting into the bed. She let the air leave her lungs. She did not respond to him. She simply let him rut in her, like an animal in heat.

Yes. She felt the pleasure building inside of her, felt his friction and his hardness and needed a release. She felt the urgency of it. His breathing was fast now. She could tell he was close to coming.

Without warning, he pushed deep into her with a groan. He held her roughly. She felt him spasm as he entered to the hilt, pumping warm come into her.

Mara heard herself gasp. She blinked, feeling her eyelashes brush against the smooth fabric. She felt disoriented as she lay there. Could this really be her enjoying being used like this? Could Dan really be doing this to her?

A thin sheen of sweat covered her body and his. She felt him lean forward, exhausted, his chest resting against the skin of her back. He laid his head between her shoulder blades as she listened to his breathing slow.

But hers did not slow. She wasn't finished. He must be able to tell she was still breathing hard. She couldn't move under the weight of him covering her, but she didn't really try. Mara let out a pleased little moan as she moved her waist, grinding against him as much as possible.

He lay like that for several minutes, allowing himself to recover completely; then she could feel him stir. He lifted his torso slightly, moving his hands up to grip her by the shoulders. His lips hovered near her ear. His hot breath brushed against her neck, and that new sensation brought her even more to attention, her body freezing in anticipation. God, she still wanted him so badly. She ached for more.

He kissed her on the shoulder, almost too briefly to notice. "Did you like that?" he asked.

No, she thought. *This can't be over yet.* She wasn't satisfied. She moaned into the bedsheets. At the same time, she thought of him. My god, what did he think of her right now? Had that brief kiss been an apology for being so rough with her, or a thank-you for allowing him to do this?

"That's not an answer," he said. "Did you like that, bitch?"

So he was still playing. She was relieved. Mara knew the answer he wanted. "Yes," she said, softly. The sound was muffled.

"What was that?" he demanded, his fingers gripping her shoulders more tightly.

"Yes," she said, speaking louder.

"Yes what?" he hissed.

"Yes...sir."

Saying that made her feel more dangerous, as if he possessed her even more now.

He took a deep breath and released it. She could tell he was satisfied with her.

"Stay perfectly still," he said.

Silently, he released his grip on her shoulders and pulled away. She felt him withdraw, sliding out of her quickly as he stood. She felt the movement of the mattress.

"Now don't fucking move," he said.

Mara obeyed, remaining perfectly still. She did not turn her head to watch him. She heard his footsteps as he crossed the room, and then the sound of a door thrown open and hangers being pushed to the side. He must be at the closet. But what could he be looking for?

The heat of his body had left her as he pulled away, making her feel instantly more naked and exposed as the cooler air hit her skin. She was suddenly unsure of herself, unsure of what she wanted, unsure of what exactly he would do next.

She lay there, unclothed, her panties dangling off of her legs. She knew that she looked like something that had been used and cast aside. That was how she felt, but somehow, right now, that was all right. She wanted to feel dirty like this.

After a few moments, he closed one of the closet doors. He was finished there. Dan crossed to the far side of the bed where he stopped. He stood still, his fingers working on something. She heard the sounds of fabric.

Whatever he was planning, Mara wanted him to be done with it. She was impatient for more, and she was ready for him to take her again. She didn't want to be dressed in some costume right now. But, of course, she also knew he would have what he wanted tonight, and there was a certain security in that. She had already felt how futile it was to struggle.

She heard him as he slowly circled around the bed, the sounds of material in his hands. Finally, he pulled her closer, standing behind her. He brought his hands to the side of her head. She could feel their strength as he brought a strip of heavy fabric across her eyes, tying it firmly behind her head.

A blindfold! As she blinked her eyes behind it, there was nothing but darkness. She still had not seen him tonight. She didn't know how she felt about this. Mara sat up, raising her hands to her face to remove it, but he was too fast for her. In an instant, he had pushed her down onto the bed, this time on her back.

Her naked breasts jiggled as she fell back. He straddled her, using his whole body weight to hold her down. He grabbed both of her arms and pinned them above her head.

"No, wait," she said. "Don't, please!"

But she didn't really mean it. She didn't want to say that word, because then it would really stop.

"If you liked that so much, let's see how you like this." His voice sounded raw and cruel now. He sounded like someone else. She loved that. She wanted to be fucked tonight by a man she didn't know.

He held her down with one arm, reaching to the side with the other. She couldn't see what he was picking up. He brought his hand closer, wrapping something around her right wrist several times before she knew what was happening. He used both hands to quickly tie it before grabbing her other arm firmly.

Mara tried to move her right arm to push him away, but she couldn't jerk it free. A silky mesh held her wrist securely in place. She recognized the texture: the flexible material of panty hose. He wasn't dressing her up. He was tying her down. This was something she hadn't expected. Soon he would have her so completely, he wouldn't even have to struggle to hold her down. Fucking her would be effortless for him. That excited her.

"No. No, stop!" she screamed. Her arm tethered in place, she bucked against him with the rest of her body, trying to throw him off balance. She thought maybe she could roll him off, but his whole weight was leveraged on top of her. It was useless. "Please, don't!"

He reached over to the other side, winding panty hose securely around her other wrist. He tied it off and sat back on her legs.

He squeezed her face with one hand, his fingers digging into her cheeks. "Quiet." he demanded.

She screamed again.

"I said quiet!" He grabbed her left nipple and twisted it hard. The pain was hot and tickling. It shot into her body with a rush. The motion was incredibly cruel and intense, and she hadn't expected it. For a moment, she couldn't respond, couldn't even breathe.

"You'll speak when I tell you to speak. Got that?" he said.

Slowly, the words registered as the pain began to dissipate. After a moment, she nodded cautiously.

He bent over her. "There's a safe in that closet. Want to give me the combination?" he asked.

She sat, thinking. If she gave him the combination now, he might stop this. She wanted to see if he was willing to keep going this time.

"I...I can't," she stammered. Mara clenched her hands into fists, preparing for him to twist her nipple again.

He slapped her once on each side of her stomach, hard and precise. As the pain flashed in front of her eyes, she thought of the safeword. She felt the lingering sting on the tender skin and knew he had left red marks behind.

"I don't know it," she said, a pleading edge to her voice.

"Well, we'll see, won't we?"

As he still sat on her legs, he leaned backward to reach for something. Mara bucked underneath him, sensing that this was a chance to resist, but she could not force him off of her. His entire weight held her legs down. She felt him wind the same fabric around one ankle, then the other, spreading her legs and tying them firmly. He climbed to the edge of the bed. She felt the movement of the mattress as he stood, then nothing.

He was silent. She knew he must be standing over her, watching. She tested her bonds, pulling on the ropes holding her wrists and ankles, but they were tied too well. She couldn't twist free.

This sensation was new. She enjoyed knowing he was looking at her as she lay there naked and helpless. She reveled in her vulnerability, but she wanted him to finish it. She arched her back and twisted on the bed, partly in an effort to break free, partly because of her pent up sexual frustration. She was wet and eager. It was freeing to realize that nothing at all was required of her. She would only have to lie there, accepting what he gave her.

It was then that she began to notice his breathing. It was faster and more labored than before, almost like panting. There was also another noise: the noise of muscles working, of skin brushing against skin.

As she listened, she realized that he was jerking off. He had tied her down and now he would humiliate her again. She would get nothing.

She went wild. She knew how hard and ready he must be. She imagined the motion of his hand stroking. With each movement on the bed, she made herself more and more excited. She tried to rub her thighs together, but couldn't. She was so close.

From the pitch of his voice, she could tell he was close, too. As he continued, she imagined the feel of his come landing on her exposed body. It would be a gesture that was dismissive, as if he cared nothing for what she wanted.

"Are you going to give me the combination?" he finally asked.

"I told you, I can't," she said.

"We'll see about that."

Suddenly, he was on top of her again. He reached underneath her and pinched her hard on the ass. "Give it to me," he said.

He slid three fingers into her pussy, curling them forward. She almost came.

"Please, no," she said.

"Have it your way, then," he said.

He was kneeling between her legs. As he spoke, he grabbed her by the hips, easily raising them up. She felt his cock brushing up against her.

Then, instantly, effortlessly, he pushed his way into her. He felt huge this time, and all consuming. Her arms and legs were held motionless by the bonds. Her hips were held up so easily against his strong body. She lay there as he took her by force again.

He pushed into her roughly twice more, and they both came. She felt it wash through her in waves as she clenched against him. Being suspended like that made her feel woozy as if she were falling, as if her stomach had jumped into her throat. He had opened her up, so utterly, like a key in a lock.

No, she thought, not like a key. Not as simple as that. It was more like a hand on a safe, slowly twisting the knob with your fingertips, listening for that muffled click as you slowly slide the lock gates into place, as you carefully divine a hidden combination.

Mara held her breath as this happened. As she exhaled, she slowly whispered several numbers.

"What?" he asked as he lowered her back down.

"The combination," she smiled. "The safe."

BACHELOR'S DESSERT

Alison Tyler

We have a standing date every Saturday night. I go out for ice cream with all of the fixings: chocolate sauce, whipped cream, jimmies. Even those little marinated cherries. Grayson stays home and preps the house for us—dims the lights, puts on the movie, starts the fire.

But when I get in line tonight, a man steps behind me. I feel him before I see him, sense his presence out of the corner of my eye. I scan the conveyer belt to see that he has a six-pack, a steak, and a bottle of whiskey.

"Bachelor's dinner," he says motioning to his groceries.

"Old married couple's dessert," I say, indicating mine.

He looks me up and down, slowly. I'm wearing my beat-up Levi's and my riding boots. A T-shirt so old and threadbare you can see the color of my bra underneath—lemon yellow, with lace on the edges. I have to use a safety pin to make the clasp hold. No mascara. No eyeliner. The blush on my cheeks is for real.

Once upon a time, I dressed up for Saturday nights. I wore

flirty sundresses and strappy sandals in the summer, velvet slacks and silken turtlenecks in the fall. I washed the barn smell off me at the end of the day and spritzed green tea perfume at the nape of my neck, under my long dark hair.

Now, I zip up the cornflower blue hoody so that I'm less exposed, and the man gives me a cocky grin and says, "I liked it better the other way."

My turn to pay saves me from having to respond. I fumble with the crumpled twenty, stuff the change in my pocket, and head out of the store as quickly as I can—home to safety, to one big bowl of ice cream that we'll share together on the sofa with two cold silver spoons, to a movie so old and familiar we can say the lines out loud. We used to fuck in front of the TV, matching the actors move for move.

Now we watch them fuck.

And we eat dessert.

But when I reach the old Buick, I can't find my car keys. I set the paper bag of groceries on the ground so I can pat my pockets, turn my sweatshirt practically inside out. My nerves are so rattled that when the stranger comes up behind me, I bite my lip to stifle a scream.

"You left these on the counter," he says, dangling my key ring in front of my eyes like a hypnotist with a pocket watch. I grab for the keys, but he holds them out of reach. He acts as if he's going to hand them over, and then taunts me once more, so I go up on tiptoe, but still can't grab the ring.

"Ask nicely," he chides, and I catch that cocky grin once more. He's toying with me, his groceries tucked into the crook of his arm, his body all long and lean in a denim jacket and faded jeans. He's not breathless the way I am. This is a game to him. But I feel the wisps of hair pulling free from my ponytail, feel the back of my T-shirt damp against my skin.

"Please," I say, as nicely as I can. I know in my head, in my heart, that what I ought to do is return to the brightly lit store and get help from the manager. Why am I playing games with a stranger? He could be dangerous. He could have a knife, or a gun. He could have dark sinister plans for me....

"Please what?"

Like *that*. The tone in his voice. I can hear exactly what those plans are. He wants to fuck me. He wants to take down my jeans and push me over the hood of my car, drive his cock into me so that I cry out. I know he's thinking of the way that cold metal will feel on my hot skin, the way his hand will find my hair, tug on it, pull my face up, make my body arch.

I look into his eyes. They're a blue that's nearly silver, like that eerie light you see both at dawn and dusk. I can't get a read from those eyes.

"Please, Sir," I say, trying my own little half a smile, "Can you help a lady out? I seem to have misplaced my keys."

I watch, a bit shell-shocked, as he slides them into his front pocket.

Does he want me to put my hand down there and reach for the keys, brush the tips of my fingers against what I can guess is the rock-hard ridge of his cock? I take a breath. I lean against the solid frame of my car. I bring one hand up to my mouth—nervous habit—and bite at my knuckles.

"You shouldn't do that," he says. "Your hands are too pretty." And he takes mine in his and pulls me to him, like we're dancing.

Jesus, I think. *How'd I get here? From old married couple's dessert, to a bachelor's dinner?* He drops his bag of groceries through the open window of the truck parked next to mine, a dark gray pickup truck that somehow suits him perfectly. Then he spins me and pushes me up against the hood. There is nothing to think about now. I know what's coming. I know what his hands are going to feel like as he pops open the fly of my 501s, yanks them down to my thighs with my panties in one single motion. I draw in my breath as he presses against me. He's still clothed, but I'm exposed. His jeans rub against my ass, and I bite down on the words that want to escape my lips, begging words.

Please fuck me. Please, fucking god, just fuck me.

I push from my mind the fact that we're out in the open, in the middle of a popular grocery store parking lot. Because we're not really that exposed, tucked off in the corner. And it's that empty hour, when most sane people are home or out on dates. Not shopping for groceries, and certainly not getting fucked in grocery store parking lots.

But I'm not getting fucked either. Not yet.

"Tell me you want this," he says, and I feel his big hand close on the back of my neck. I shudder all over. I can't speak. I'm so damn wet, and so damn scared, and every dark desire, every unspoken fantasy I've ever dared to have seems to be poised right here, on the tip of my tongue.

"Say it."

His hand tightens, but I am frozen, speechless. A car sweeps by, keeps going. We've gone unnoticed. Or we've passed as a couple of lovers out kissing in the dark. Except we're not kissing. He's got his cock pressed against me through one layer of denim, and he's waiting for me to speak.

At least, he was.

He's not waiting anymore. The man pulls back just enough to pop his own fly, and then I feel the heat of him against my naked skin. I've waited too long to say what I want. Now, he's going to take what he wants.

The head of his cock presses into me, and he feels the instant wetness envelope him. His groan makes me shiver. He doesn't loosen his grip on my neck, but now his hand slips around so he's holding the front of my throat. Oh, holy fuck, I've never felt anything so sexy.

He thrusts into me once, twice, hard and fast, and tears leak from my eyes. But I am not prepared for what he does next. With his cock all glossy and wet from my pussy, he pulls back, and then I feel the pressure at my asshole, and I stiffen, but he doesn't hesitate. There is no "Tell me you want this" now. There is only his cock, driving in hard, not waiting, not going slow.

He's fucking my ass in the parking lot of a Lucky's and I am going to melt into an oil slick like the one right next to my feet, rainbow lit and shimmery in the halo of saffron from the streetlights.

The safety pin holding my bra together digs into my back as he slams into me. The car metal bites my skin. I am demolished as he lets go of my throat, as he grinds one big hand down my body and presses his thumb to my clit so I come when he comes, as he empties himself into me.

There is the smell of exhaust and dark wet asphalt.

No perfume has ever smelled sweeter.

"They were out of jimmies," I tell Grayson when I get home—rumpled, breathless. Does he notice? "I had to drive to two other stores."

He pats the sofa at his side. There in the den of darkness, waiting, fire crackling.

I breathe in deep. He's got steak cooking. I can hear the sizzle.

EXTREME DOGGING

Dylan Reed

The sedan pulled up at about eleven forty-five to where the big skinhead sat on a bus stop bench reading a *True Detective*. He was about six four and burly, shaved headed, with a couple days' growth. He was not wearing a jacket, just a tight white T-shirt, snug faded blue jeans, and combat boots.

The redhead in the backseat was packed into a loose summer dress of thin black cotton; her braless tits were halfway visible at the edges of the spaghetti straps, and with her legs held partway open, the cuckolder could see the lacy tops of her sheer black stockings where they hitched to her black garter belt. She also wore high heels, which would have looked amazingly fetching on her five-ten frame if she'd been standing up. Her pretty, pale, lightly freckled face was ringed with a cascading mane of copper hair.

"How's it going," he said.

She nodded. "I'm Vanessa."

No other conversation was necessary. The guy did not introduce himself. He got into the backseat.

The redhead kissed him. It was a wet kiss on her part, and a dry one on his; he didn't respond but kept his lips tight together. Vanessa got the message: maybe this was some kind of gay public sex no kissing rule. Either way was fine with her.

She tucked her long legs under her perfect ass and cuddled up against him, taking his hand and leaning heavily on his great bulk; she let her hand rest casually in his lap, not far from his cock, which was stiffening.

Mark hit the gas and headed for the nearest onramp. As her husband drove, Vanessa gently kissed the cuckolder's ear, letting her tongue laze out to tease it; she let her breath come harder than it normally would have—not because she was really out of breath, but because she liked to feel the cuckolder's cock stirring against her, and she knew from experience that one of the surefire ways to get a man hard in moments is for a woman to begin panting up against him. There were a thousand other ways, but she liked this one. It worked flawlessly.

"Have you ever gotten a blowjob on the freeway?" Vanessa asked.

The cuckolder shook his head.

"Hey, you two," said Mark nervously. "None of that, now. No below-the-waist till we get to the Point. You know the rules!"

"Fuck the rules," said Vanessa.

"Yes, Ma'am," said Mark, chastened. The car seat squeaked as his hips worked absently up and down.

She winked in the dark at the cuckolder; she smiled and he did not smile back. He was looking at her, his eyes roving over her tits, her face, her long legs tucked under a perfect ass.

"It won't be long," she said.

The cuckolder let his arm drape around her, caressing the side of her breasts as she ran her open palm over his stiffening cock.

It was ten minutes before Mark pulled into the parking space. That short drive, in fact, was one of the two biggest reasons this particular cuckolder had been lucky enough to get Vanessa tonight—ease of access. The other was—

"Oh, my," said Vanessa. "You weren't lying."

"Not by much," admitted the cuckolder as Vanessa's hand, which had slid down his pants during the ride, moved gently up and down. There was a *screech-chunk* sound as Mark set the parking break.

"Take a walk, Mark," Vanessa said.

Mark looked over the back of the seat, watching his wife stroke the skinhead's big cock.

"I said take a walk," Vanessa said as she lowered her face to his crotch. "You can watch like all the others."

Mark got out of the car and slammed it behind him. He clicked the electronic lock and the sedan chirped. It would keep some overzealous voyeur from trying to hop into the action, which occasionally happened, though Mark was fairly sure the cuckolder could take care of anyone who tried anything too forward—including him. Mark's cock stiffened as he stood a few feet away; a few other guys were standing at respectful distances for now, creeping closer. One already had his cock out.

"What's your story, man?" he asked.

"I'm watching, same as you."

"She your girlfriend?"

"Wife," he said.

"No kidding! That's fucking awesome. Hey, you think I could—"

"No," said Mark.

"Of course, man. Had to ask, man. Don't mind if I watch, though?"

"That's what we're here for."

Mark resisted the urge to pull his own cock out just yet—there'd be a long, sweet suck before he saw her riding him. He knew it from experience—always ten minutes of suck, and at least ten of fuck, depending on the guy. The Point was the only place where you could get away with half an hour in the public eye without attracting law enforcement attention. He stood a few feet away and watched as the couple in the car got down to business.

Inside the car, the windows were steaming up. The cuckolder reached out for Vanessa and pulled the top of her dress between her tits, revealing perfect breasts with pale nipples, freckles dusting the former, goose bumps on the latter. He teased the dress there and held it, bent down and sucked one nipple into his own mouth. He caressed the other breast with his open hand as she relaxed into the seat and let her arms laze over the back of it. The cuckolder made love to her tits and Vanessa reached up to untie her dress at the back of her neck. The dress fell forward, giving the cuckolder greater access to her tits; he made love to them hungrily as she reached for his cock. As she ran her open palm over his bulge, she stroked the fingers of her other hand through his almost-skinhead hair; he moved from one breast to the other as his hand went up her dress.

He knew already that she was bare and wet; he could smell her, even over the lingering scent of her husband's sweat and the chemical smell of a car too-recently cleaned. The upholstery of this bucket probably got a regular workout, the cuckolder knew.

As he put his hand up her dress, she went wide there on the seat, spreading her legs for him. His hand glided up and down the inside of her perfect freckled thigh, nearing her cunt; he got his fingers up against her, teasing her slit. He felt her melting onto his hand as he began to tease her open. She was snug, a practiced tightness, and as slick as cunts can be. He put two fingers deep inside her and his thumb against her clit. She moaned. She could feel her G-spot swelling, and if his skills at finger-fucking were any indication, he could too; he started to press against it, working the pads of his fingers over her swelling inside bulge as her cunt juiced still more.

As he finger-fucked her smoothly, he put his face right up to hers, and she parted her lips to be kissed.

But the cuckolder didn't kiss her; their only kiss so far had been the abortive one when he got in. Vanessa loved to be kissed, almost as much as she loved to suck cock. Vanessa leaned forward slightly to press her lips to his, and he pulled back. His eyes narrowed and held hers tightly; she fell into them desperately with a sharp surge of abstract pleasure: "Whores don't get kissed, they get fucked," she whispered.

"That's right," he said, and that was plenty to send her whimpering into the stratosphere, her cunt giving a clench around his fingers as she felt more like a whore than she already did. Vanessa loved to be kissed, but she loved even more to be treated like the type of girl who didn't get kissed.

"Well, I've got to do something with my mouth," she whispered excitedly.

The cuckolder slid his fingers out of her, brought them up to her mouth and eased his hand into her cascade of red hair. He gripped her hair tightly as he forced his fingers in, and Vanessa whimpered. She suckled obediently, licking her cunt off his fingers. As she did, he used both hands to guide her face down to his crotch. His pants were already open, so it was easy to get his jockeys down and take his cock into her mouth. He was even bigger at close range. Vanessa's lipsticked mouth went working up his shaft, licking precum from his tip and sliding down to tongue his balls. She started sucking with mounting eagerness, her lips circling his shaft as she pumped up and down on him.

After a few minutes she came up for air, panting.

"Now don't dare come in my mouth," she said.

"Don't like the taste?" he asked.

"I love the taste," she said. "But I wanna fuck."

"Don't worry," said the cuckolder. Vanessa's mouth went back down on his cock and started working eagerly over him; her tongue lavished affection on the underside as she tried to gauge his arousal from his moans. Promises, promises: the guy could still shoot on her face and never know it was coming... and then she'd be left making cell phone calls at midnight. No one wanted that.

Outside the car, Mark stood smoking, while a growing group of men edged in, a couple wearing trench coats, some in sweats, still others with their peckers out and visible. Mark didn't do a thing; he just stood there, his cock erect. He glanced at his watch. His breathing quickened.

Vanessa suckled precum off the cuckolder's cockhead. One hand held his shaft down near the base; with the other, she reached down and began to frig herself.

"God, I'm fucking wet," she said.

"So do something about it."

"I think I will," she smiled, and climbed up onto her knees on the seat. She planted one knee on each side of him and slid herself down on him, using one hand to guide his cock to her pussy. She slid it up and down, looking into his eyes; his lips were tight, and she wanted very badly to kiss him. She felt a wave of erotic tension from knowing she could not. She worked his cockhead into her and said, "Fuck!" as she slid down onto him. He was big; he fit into her only with effort, making her feel fuller than she'd felt in ages. This position made her feel tighter, she knew from experience—or maybe it was just that she liked to use this position in situations where she could choose her cocks like a poor girl at a smorgasbord...and she always chose the big ones.

Mark was startled when the big dark car arrived; the masturbators all around him, seasoned professionals, yelped and scattered like cockroaches. Mark just stood there, watching, and when the plainclothes cop got out and pointed at him, he said, "Oh, fuck," and then he reached into his pocket and obediently hit the button.

The door locks clicked; the cop reached in and hit his red lights, then opened the door before Vanessa could climb off the cuckolder. In fact, little had changed inside the car; Vanessa still rode him and he never even stopped thrusting.

The cop badged them.

"You mind stepping out of the car?" he said.

"We're just having a little harmless fun," said Vanessa.

"Please step out of the car. Both of you."

Vanessa didn't climb off the cuckolder; she was still riding him, her tits bare, her breasts brushing his face. He didn't move to change positions, either.

"Please, officer. Let us finish. I'll make it worth your while..." Vanessa turned a little toward him so he could get a better look at her tits; the cop appraised them eagerly.

"I mean really worth your while," she said. "Just let me finish."

"Officer, please," said Mark, rushing up to him. "This is my car."

"Your car? Who are you?"

"Her husband," said Mark. "We...we meant no harm."

"*We meant no harm?* Is this some kind of thing you people do?"

In the cop's car, the police scanner chirped and crackled: *104 in progress. 17 on West Lincoln. 713 in Durden Heights.*

Vanessa was riding the cuckolder with greater ferocity; she worked her pussy up and down on his cock so that the cop could see his shaft outlined against the door lights. The cop could smell her. In fact, Mark could smell her, too; the pungent scent of female sex was wafting out of the car.

"I'm afraid so, officer—"

"It's detective," said the cop.

"Detective, I'm sorry. Yes, this is a thing we do. We meant no harm."

The cop made a disgusted noise. "You drive your wife up to the Point to fuck with strangers?"

"Yes," said Mark breathlessly.

The cop squared his shoulders, growled: "You probably lick her clean afterward!"

"Yes, sometimes—" Mark began.

"You probably lick him clean afterward!"

"Yes, if he wants it—" gasped Mark.

The cop's voice had been getting swiftly louder, and now he cried out in a bellow: "You probably warm him up for her!"

"Not this one...but, yes, sometimes—"

"You disgusting little—"

Vanessa rode the cuckolder, crying out as she said, "Oh, god, I think I'm going to cum.... I'm going to turn around and sit on you, jack me off while I ride you, please, baby?"

Vanessa lifted herself off the cuckolder, worked herself around, crowded herself up against the ceiling, steadying herself on the front seat. She spread her legs and nuzzled her cunt up to the cuckolder's cockhead; at the last moment before taking him into her, she said, "You don't mind, do you, detective? I don't want to get our guest in trouble. I'll still make it worth your while, if you..."

"That won't be necessary," the detective said. "You kids go right ahead and fuck. Do her fucking ass for all I care." He pointed at Mark. "It's you got some explaining to do, son. You warm your wife's 'boyfriends' up for her?"

"Sometimes, Sir, yes—"

"Does that make your little pecker hard?"

"It does, Sir, yes—"

"Then show me," snapped the detective.

Trembling, Mark obeyed. He unfastened his belt and unzipped his pants; he took his cock out, displaying it to the detective. It was hard.

The scanner chirped: *213 in progress, South Pendergast. 424 on Washington.*

The cop was almost screaming: "You ever warm them up without her?"

Mark bleated: "No, Sir, that would be—"

"That would be what?" thundered the detective. "Show me what it would be, you little bitch!" He pointed angrily to the pink triangle lapel pin affixed to his trench coat, swept the coat open and reached for his belt buckle.

"Show me!" he shouted.

"Y-yes, Sir," whimpered Mark, dropping to his knees and crawling to the detective. Vanessa let out a cry of pleasure as the cop opened up his pants pulled a half-hard dick out of boxer shorts with badges on them. Mark's mouth enveloped the thick cockhead and started working up and down as his eyes turned up toward the cop. Without being ordered to, he took a deep breath, nudged the cockhead against his throat, and swallowed easily, taking the cop's prick all the way into him. He came up for air and slid his tongue from cockhead to base and then to balls; he came up and started sucking again, pumping it down into his throat and then bobbing up and down on it. His eyes took in the sight of the cop's cruel face; he was grinning savagely as his cock got sucked.

"Yeah, see what that is? It's smoking pole, you little cocksucker, whether it tastes like your wife's cunt or my boyfriend's fucking asshole. And you like it, don't you, pal?"

Mark whimpered.

"I said you like it?" Mark nodded obediently, never letting the cop's prick leave his mouth. "Yeah, you do it pretty well for someone who needs a skirt to get his cock fix, son. You know what they say down in Q-town—married men give the best head."

"Yes, Sir," panted Mark as he worked his way from head to balls, caressing the shaft with his tongue and rubbing it all over his face.

In the car, Vanessa was crying out wildly. The cop leaned into the car and said, "You kids all right?"

"Just fine, Sir," Vanessa whimpered.

The cuckolder was stroking Vanessa's clit, his fingers pressed up alongside his big prick. She rode him facing out, moaning wildly as she lifted herself halfway off his cock and then slammed down onto him.

The police scanner chirped and bleated: *445 in progress. 17 at Western Park.*

The detective turned back to Mark. "From the looks of it, you don't mind it one bit—nobody's putting a gun to your head." He swept his trench back to reveal his—just to remind everyone he had one.

"No, Sir," said Mark, slurping audibly.

"Now stroke it off."

Mark slid his mouth up to the detective's cockhead and put his hand around the shaft.

"Not mine!" howled the cop. "Yours, cocksucker. Stroke

your dick off on my fucking shoes. You better aim, or you'll be eating dirt."

Vanessa cried out, moaning, "Come in me. Come inside me, baby. Shoot it in me."

Mark lowered his cock to his hand and began to stroke rapidly while his mouth worked up and down on the detective's cock. As he mounted toward orgasm, he could barely suck; uncontrolled moans were coming from his mouth, and so he put his other hand around the detective's shaft and started pumping.

"Yeah, you can pretend I'm making you do this all you want, just like you pretend she's making you do it...but you're gonna spooge my fucking shoes before I fill your fucking mouth, aren't you? Don't you fucking dare shoot on the ground, pig, or you'll eat dirt, so help me god, you'll eat a cumload's worth of dirt—"

Mark cried out, leaning over and aiming his cock at the detective's big black shoes. Cum erupted from his cockhead, spewing over the black leather in streaming spurts. Some squirted into the dirt. Mark looked up at the detective in guilty anticipation.

"Clean later," said the cop. "Now make me come."

Mark put his mouth back where it belonged and started stroking the cop rhythmically, feeling his hips pump as he got closer. Inside, Vanessa cried out louder than ever, and the cuckolder erupted in a thundering roar of orgasm; the cop's prick spurted cum and Mark suckled on it hungrily, his throat muscles working as he swallowed every stream.

"Now clean!" snapped the cop.

Mark licked the cop all over, then lowered himself to the big black shoes and started licking. It was hard to see where every drop of cum had hit, so the cop helpfully pulled out his pocket flashlight and shined it down on Mark.

"You missed a spurt," he said.

Mark lapped it up.

In the backseat, Vanessa and the cuckolder were still moaning, and Vanessa was performing much the same service on the cuckolder that Mark performed on the detective's shoes. Mark looked into the car and saw Vanessa's face bobbing up and down in the cuckolder's crotch; the detective reached out and slammed the door as Mark put away the cop's prick and delicately zipped his pants.

The scanner crackled. *Unspecified disturbance at the Point, nearby unit please respond.*

Unit 226 on the way from Placer Canyon, ETA in five.

"Keep it real, cocksucker," growled the cop. He walked over to his sedan and climbed in. He started the car and threw it into reverse as Mark sprinted for the driver's seat. They raced each other down the mountain.

As Mark took the curves at high speed, Vanessa finished cleaning up the cuckolder, put his cock away, and fixed her dress. She sat facing him in his lap, leaning close.

"Same place okay?"

"That's fine. That wasn't what I expected."

"You posted 'up for anything.'"

"Yeah," said the cuckolder. "That'll teach me."

He kissed her, open-mouthed, with lots of tongue.

A GUY SHE'S NEVER MET

Zach Addams

It's not like I thought I would end up this way. On the contrary, before I had a girlfriend I always thought I'd be possessive—I would never want to share. I thought when I was madly in love, when I loved a woman more than life itself, I would keep her close, never letting another man near her for fear of losing her. Now I know different. I've got the hottest girlfriend in the world, and I'm crazy for her. But as much as I love fucking her, and she loves fucking me, it's just as hot to watch her spread to get fucked by a guy she's never met.

That's the key to what makes my dick so fucking hard; this isn't someone she's picked out in the usual manner. Oh, she picked him out, all right...in that special way that, I'm betting, plenty of women would like to pick their men but never get to, because they don't have boyfriends as cool as me. Maria looked through hundreds, maybe thousands, of pictures of guys' dicks, without the option to look at their faces. I kept them all catalogued in a spreadsheet for her, so that I could match them to pictures of guys' faces and be prepared when I met with them.

I had already looked through and discarded the guys who failed to follow instructions. What I needed, as stated in the personal ad I wrote, was

> Well-hung studly guy, 20-40, ripped, cut or uncut, to fuck my girlfriend in all holes. Any race. Please be fit and hung. She is 25, brunette, very oral, receptive. Include high-res JPG of your face, one of your dick, and then a picture of both. If we proceed, paperwork will be expected.

The key was to know that the dick was real, the face was real, and they more or less went together. Otherwise, fortysomething guys would send in a picture of themselves at twenty-two, a JPG of Jeff Stryker's cock, and leave us having been had in more ways than one.

I included seven JPGs of Maria, from the waist down or from behind. In one she had her legs spread, gorgeous smooth shaved cunt exposed. In another she was on hands and knees, her long, lustrous black hair streaming down her back, her legs spread wide and her cheeks parted to show her perfect pink asshole. Another showed her from the side, from her tits to her thighs—gorgeous. In others she was touching herself. It was a nice assortment of pictures; if I'd seen it myself, I would have thought "Bullshit—porn star." But she's for real. She's very much for real.

There were thousands of responses; perhaps two hundred guys could follow instructions. Maria and I had a date to have her look through the cock-only images. The understanding was that she would pick out the guys she wanted me to verify and consider inviting over—not the guys, so much, but the *cocks*, with no concern over whether the guys would be good looking, kind, gentle, or sexy; she would not worry about whether they would smell good, taste good, or be losing their hair. That would all be my concern. She would focus on one thing and one thing only: *Do I want this dick sliding into me?* Every time I thought about it, my own dick would get hard, and fucking fast.

We made the selection one Friday night; I made her dinner, poured her wine, complimented her on her dress and told her how good she'd look out of it. We had a long, slow, lush dinner with several more refills of wine and a lot of deep conversation. Then I kissed her, took her hand and led her from the table to the desk. I sat her down, poured her more wine, and put on soft music.

I called up the file with dick photos, pulled over a chair and sat down next to her, my eyes roving from my girlfriend to the cocks of her potential lovers.

She looked nervous at first, but quickly settled into the task.

She sipped red wine. She lingered on each cock, her eyes slowly sliding up and down their fleshy expanses on the twenty-inch computer monitor.

She made some comments. "I like this one. Nice big thick head. Don't you think that would feel nice going into me? He'd have to work at it."

I breathed hard, leaning in to agree.

She took little sips of wine as she considered each one and then slowly paged to the next. "This one's far too long... If he was thicker, I'd like that, but...you know how I like them wide."

"I do," I responded.

She sipped. "Oh, my...this next one looks especially thick... I'm not sure I could do anal with him...and you know I want to do *everything*."

When we'd first started the negotiation, she hadn't wanted to fuck. The original plan was that after meeting the guy and talking with him extensively, she might suck his cock, but never go all the way. Then as we talked more, it became clear that what I really wanted was this—"all holes," with a stranger, a guy she'd never met. Gradually Maria came around to my way of thinking. Now she was getting as turned on by the idea as I was. I could see her nipples, as she was braless in the thin flowered minidress, stiffening and showing through the fabric. As she leaned forward in the chair I could see the skirt riding up her thighs and knew underneath she was wet.

I had weeded out the small ones; "Well-hung" has many interpretations, but she knows it when she sees it. She had lots to consider. Between lingering, longing looks at the images of strangers' dicks, Maria would look over at me and smile, seeing my red face, my lips slightly parted, my breath coming quickly. She would lean over and kiss me periodically, and ask my opinion on cocks.

"Do you think this one could fuck my tits? Look at that head... Wouldn't that look nice shooting cum all over my face?"

"Yeah," I panted. "That would look good."

"Oh, this one... I like that he's so long... You know how I love to have my cervix pounded. When I'm in the mood. You're going to help me get in the mood, aren't you, darling?"

"Definitely," I breathed.

"Oh, wow...this one's nice. Something about the curve. I think it would hit me in all the right places...."

Finally, I couldn't stand it anymore. I leaned in and kissed Maria hungrily; my hands roved all over her and began to unfasten the front of her dress. She kissed me back but then gently pushed me away when I began to pull her dress off of her.

"Please...please, darling. I've got work to do. I'm trying to pick out a stranger's cock to fuck me. There are so many of them. If I don't keep working, I'll never decide which ones I want."

"You think you might want more than one?" I asked breathlessly.

"Of course," said Maria. "Who knows? Three, four, five... maybe ten. I don't have to restrict myself, do I?"

I shook my head. "Then keep looking, and let me lick you."

"All right," she sighed. "But don't distract me."

"I love you, baby," I breathed.

"I know," she said wryly.

My dick gave a surge.

Normally, she would have given me the usual response—she loved me too. But these weren't normal circumstances. Her detachment, her fixation, her total obsession with cock, or *cocks*—other men's cocks, and an abstract quantity—made me fucking unbelievably hot. And I already knew that she loved me; otherwise, she'd never be able to do it this way.

She spread her legs, cocking her knees over the sides of the chair. The skirt came up easily; it was loose, and she wasn't wearing a thing underneath. I moaned softly and went down on my knees, pressing my mouth to her cunt. She was smooth and slick and juicy. I began to lick eagerly.

I worked her clit with my tongue as she breathed rhythmically, sinking into the pleasure. She continued to comment on the dicks she was viewing. "This one has too much shaft, not enough head... I want something big at the top, don't you agree?" She'd guide my face up from between her thighs and make me look at the dick that might fuck her, and agree or disagree with her—usually agree.

One time, I did disagree with her, when she nudged me away from my task after saying, "I could never do this one, darling. I think he'd positively rip me in two...don't you think?"

She guided me up, made me look at a mammoth prick with foreskin pulled back, head purpled with arousal and drizzling precum. I caught my breath.

"I think it's perfect," I said.

"Really?" she said. "You'd have to lick me so good and get me really turned on to take it...."

"I would," I begged. "I promise."

"All right, then. We'll bookmark this one," she sighed. She pushed my face down between her thighs, and after that she didn't have many comments or questions—just long, low moans as she built toward orgasm.

She was supposed to pick a dozen, maybe, or half a dozen to choose from. She settled on one. It was the particularly outlandish uncut cock with dripping precum. I thought at first it'd prove to be a hoax—and I can't help but think maybe Maria did, as well. But it was not. When I went back to my spreadsheet, there he was: a good-looking thirtysomething black man, with a JPG of his face and one of both his face and dick. He was real.

Surely he'd prove boorish, unsuitable for the task. I met with him at a local pub, not too close to the house. His name was David. He was six-foot-four, soft spoken and charming. He explained he was uncut because he'd been raised in Guatemala by hippies. He brought his paperwork—testing for all the nasty bugs that might make this venture risky. He wanted to verify that this was something my girlfriend had initiated.

"Well...I initiated it," I said. "But I think she's as into it as I am at this point."

"I have a hard time believing that," said David with a grin; he could tell I was crazed for the idea. "You have a picture of her face?"

I'd brought one, a print, hard copy, something that couldn't be duplicated or distributed. I pushed it over to him: Maria in a bikini, pretty as can be with full tits all but popping out of rainbow spandex.

"Holy crap," he said. "She's gorgeous. And you'll be watching?"

I nodded.

"But not participating."

"Unless she wants me to," I said. "She won't." It was part of the dream—that I could be summoned at any time to help her out, to get her off, provide her a second cock, to hold her while he fucked her, or hold her open for him. But even that would be denied me.

"I'm going to jerk off, though. Do you mind that?"

"No."

"That's a relief."

"All right," he said. "Obviously, I'm game."

I pushed across an index card with our address, a date, a time.

"I'll be there," he said.

"How would you like her?" I asked.

"Excuse me?"

"Dressed up...naked...lingerie... I mean, you won't be going out or anything, but if you've got a costume you're partial to..."

"She like high heels?"

"Loves them."

"And stockings? Garter belt?"

"But of course."

"She have a name?"

"I'd rather you didn't call her by it," I said nervously.

David grinned.

"No reason to know it, then, is there? And she won't know mine?"

"Right."

"I'll see you Saturday."

Maria greets him at the door dressed for action: black lace garter belt, black seamed stockings, black six-inch high heels. Her perfect tits are bare. The neighbors might be scandalized, if David's great size didn't shield her from their gaze. He's wearing jeans and a dress shirt, black leather boots.

She kisses him at the door, on the lips, full of heat and lots of tongue. She leads him into the living room, where he accepts a beer from me and plants his mammoth bulk on the big white sofa. It's summer, so the sun's still out; the sliding glass door is open to the backyard and there's a nice breeze coming through as, without conversation, Maria lowers herself to her knees and gets to work on his belt.

"Getting right to business, huh?" grins David, and takes a pull from his beer as she gets his pants open. He's wearing cotton boxers; the fly comes open easily but his dick's so big she has to work to get it through. I watch as Maria takes a deep breath of its scent and eases back the foreskin. She exposes its purple head, making a little savoring sound as she makes it clear how much she wants it.

"I've never sucked an uncut man before," Maria says.

My own dick hardens instantly as her tongue begins to slide up and down on David's prick.

The breeze from the backyard blows in as David relaxes into the sofa and sighs. Maria licks her way down to the base of his shaft, then back to the head; then she opens wide and swallows him, struggling as she gets it to the back of her throat. She comes back up for air and then bobs up and down on him, her mascara running down her cheeks. David glances over at me and grins.

I take my cock out and stroke it slowly. David gathers up

Maria's hair to give me and him a better view of her beautiful face as she works her mouth wetly up and down on his cock, drooling everywhere. Her tongue lolls out and works all around his cockhead, licking off the precum. The way she's turned, on her hands and knees with her ass toward me, I can see her legs spread wide, exposing her cunt. Five minutes ago, my face was between her perfect thighs, licking her, stroking her, fluffing her. The taste of her cunt is strong in my mouth. I can almost feel her clit against my tongue as she comes up slowly, spreads her pretty stocking-clad legs, and gets on the couch.

She helps David off with his shirt, exposing a big, ripped chest with tattoos. His pants go easily down his legs until they're gathered, with his boxers, around his ankles. She leans forward and suckles on his nipples softly, then kisses him as she reaches back and draws his foreskin down again, guiding his exposed cockhead to her sex. She works it between her lips and finds her hole; then, moaning, she sits down on it.

It takes a nice long time for her to work his cock into her; he's so fucking big that I can see her straining to take it. She might have an easier time if she added a little lube, but I know she likes it tight; she likes to work to get her cunt fucked. The head, in particular, seems to stretch her, but even once that's inside she's got to move her hips slowly around to push herself onto it. Once her pussy is stretched halfway down his shaft, she runs her hand all over it, feeling how full she is. She looks into his eyes and starts to fuck herself on top of him, kissing him periodically, tenderly, on the lips.

As they fuck, David easily kicks off his shoes, his pants, his boxers, even his socks—leaving him naked, fucking my girlfriend.

I stroke my cock but have to work not to shoot already. David glances over at me now and then, but Maria is completely ignoring me, which only makes me hotter. I watch as her slowly fucking strokes take her lower on David's shaft, her cunt expanding to accommodate him, stretching to accept his length and girth. She's crying out before five minutes have passed; then I see her fucking rapidly, reaching down to rub her clit.

She cries out wildly, jerking uncontrollably. She always comes fast in this position; it's why she chose it to start with. She wants to come, and come, and come, the way I begged her to—and when I see her writhing on top of David, I know she's just getting started.

After she's climaxed the first time, she works herself off of him with slight difficulty and gets back down on her knees before him. David's groaning softly as her mouth returns to his dick; she sucks his cock more eagerly than ever, savoring the taste of her own cunt. She looks up at him and begs, "Don't come yet...please don't come yet. I want you everywhere," and she doesn't have to spell it out—he knows what she means. If he can hold out, he'll get that sweet ass, the one he probably jerked off to when looking at the JPGs of Maria's perfect rear view. David chuckles and nods, and when Maria's good and sated, his cock slick with drool again, she lets him guide her back onto the couch, spreading her wide as he positions himself between her opened legs.

He guides his cock back into her and slides it home. He starts fucking her as she moans; he gets her wrists and pins her down tight against the couch to give him better leverage. He starts fucking her slowly at first; within a minute, he's pounding her to her steadily mounting cries. He leans in and sucks her nipples as he fucks her; then he leans back on his haunches and grabs her tightly, lifting her up and down on his bulk. She comes again, her body twisting and writhing. She doesn't look over at me, but David does.

When she's done coming the second time, she whispers, "Fuck me doggy-style...and then do my ass." He helps her to her hands and knees on the big assortment of pillows I've arrayed for the occasion. She spreads her legs. He gets behind her. In this position, I know from experience, she's really tight. He has to work to get his cock back into her, but then, she's nice and wide and open.

He starts to fuck her, from behind; he's pointed her face right at me so I can see her reaction as she's getting pounded. I want to see her penetrated, so I come around and lean in close; I can smell her cunt, his cock, the sweat of both of them. David reaches out, grabs my hair, pulls me close to where his cock slides into Maria.

This is the last thing I was expecting, but the feel of his bulky hand on the back of my head makes my cock throb. Maria looks back and takes an obvious thrill in seeing me forced to watch her getting fucked; when David releases me with a grin, I look up meekly and kneel nearby as Maria's eyes center on my face.

"Go get the lube," he tells me.

Nervously, I rise; I've left the lube on the coffee table, close to them. I hold it out for him; he shakes his head and I obediently open the bottle. I pour it between Maria's cheeks; I put some on my hand and gingerly reach down her back and rub the tight bud of her asshole, careful not to get any lube on Maria's expensive garter belt or to touch David's cock.

"Thanks," he says. "Now you can sit down again."

I return to my chair and start stroking myself again as Maria looks up at me and locks eyes. I watch as David eases his cock out of her, guides it to her asshole. She begins moaning crazily as he works to stretch her around him. What he doesn't know is that I've already prepped her...my tongue spent half an hour in Maria's rear entrance earlier, fluffing her for him, getting her ready to open for his cock. Even so, he's big and she's petite...so tight she has to struggle for it. He finally succeeds in getting his cockhead into her ass, and she gasps as it pops in. I watch the rapture on her face as she slowly takes it. He reaches out and grabs her hair; his other hand rests lazily on one asscheek, holding her open wide for his long strokes. He starts to fuck her gently as she moans, her hand going down between her legs and rubbing rapidly. She starts crying out, rhythmically, pumping herself back onto David's cock as he fucks her in the ass.

And then she comes, louder than ever, her whole body jerking and shuddering as pleasure takes her over. "Come inside me," she begs as she climaxes, and David grunts and starts fucking faster. It isn't another thirty seconds before he grabs her hair more tightly, making her cry out as he cries out. He comes hard inside her asshole, and Maria moans. I can tell from the look on her face that she can feel it, slick up inside her.

When his cock softens and pops out, he helps her onto the couch and I hand him another beer. Maria spreads her legs and he fingers her for a while before she stops him, kisses him, and smiles.

David doesn't need to be asked; he chuckles, finishes his beer, and gets his clothes on. Maria walks him to the door, kisses him as he leaves.

She shuts the door behind him, comes over to where I'm sitting. She leans down and plants her mouth on mine; I can taste the stranger's cock.

"Thank you, baby," she says.

"Did you like it?"

She smiles.

"A little bit too much," she says. "Want to look at JPGs?"

I catch my breath. I nod.

She leads me to the computer, where I watch her page through cocks.

I always thought I'd be possessive—I never thought I'd like to share. But now I know different; my favorite night is when my girlfriend gets fucked by a man she's never met. And she wouldn't have it any other way.

ABOUT THE AUTHORS

ZACH ADDAMS is a San Francisco queer who has written erotica for the anthologies *Love Under Foot*, *Three-Way* and *Master*, as well as GoodVibes.com and Eros-Zine.com. He wants a girlfriend and a boyfriend but has so far succeeded only in being a total slut.

FELIX D'ANGELO has been writing erotica for years, but only made his first sale to Violet Blue's *Sweet Life 2: Erotic Fantasies for Couples*. His work has since appeared on her Open Source Sex podcast and at GoodVibes.com, as well as in *Best Bondage Erotica*. He says the research for this story was oodles of fun.

JANINE ASHBLESS (janineashbless.blogspot.com) has two collections of erotic fantasy, fairy and paranormal stories, *Cruel Enchantment* and *Dark Enchantment*, and three erotic fantasy novels: *Divine Torment*, *Burning Bright* and *Wildwood*. Her short stories have appeared in anthologies by Black Lace and Cleis.

KAT BLACK is a mild-mannered aspiring romance writer by day, mistress of wicked words by night. She is an enthusiastic newcomer to the steamy world of erotica following the success of her first sexy short story, which won runner-up in the Vulgari Prize for Erotic Fiction 2008.

ANDREA DALES's (cyvarwydd.com) stories have appeared in a slew of anthologies and magazines. With coauthors, she has sold novels to Virgin Books and even more short stories. She has lived in Wales and based Pencraig on an actual castle that was saved from development by rare bats.

JAN DARBY is a lawyer and a storyteller, writing legal documents by day and lighthearted erotic romance by night. Her short stories have appeared at Ruthiesclub.com and Forthegirls.com and she has also published two novella-length erotic-romance romps.

AMANDA FOX is a wife, mother, fitness fanatic, writer, teacher, artist and hopeful humanitarian. As one half of a vanilla/chocolate love affair that has spanned more than twenty years, her writing focuses mainly on interracial relationships. She'd love you to visit her at Foxtales.ca, Cleansheets or the Erotic Woman.

KAY JAYBEE (kayjaybee.me.uk) wrote the erotic anthology *The Collector*. A regular contributor to the website oystersandchocolate.com, Kay also has a number of stories published by Cleis Press, Black Lace, Xcite Books, Mammoth Books and Penguin.

D. L. KING is the editor of *The Sweetest Kiss* and *Where the Girls Are*, and also publishes the review site, Erotica Revealed. Find her stories in *Girl Crazy, Best Women's Erotica 09* and *Best Lesbian Erotica 08 & 2010*, among others. She's published two novels.

JUDE MASON writes in a variety of genres and adores stretching the boundaries. The bulk of her work has been about D/s and femdom, but she enjoyed straying into fetish, pulp fiction, m/m or f/f, and sci-fi, among others. She has work in print, ebook form and audio.

N. T. MORLEY (ntmorley.com) is the author of sixteen published novels of erotic dominance and submission, including *The Parlor*, *The Limousine*, *The Appointment*, *The Visitor*, *The Nightclub*, and trilogies *The Castle*, *The Office* and *The Library*. Morley edited a double anthology, *MASTER/slave*, and has appeared in more than fifty anthologies.

EMILIE PARIS is the author of *Valentine*. Her short stories have appeared in anthologies including *Naughty Stories from A to Z*, volumes *1* & *3*, in *Sweet Life 1* & *2* and *Taboo*, and on the website goodvibes.com.

DYLAN REED is a bi San Francisco genderqueer with a serious thing for edgy midnight public misbehavior. Though several pseudonymous stories of Dylan's have hit the net, this is Dylan's first foray into hot bi cuckolding porn.

Erotica by **TERESA NOELLE ROBERTS** has appeared in *Pleasure Bound*, *Best Women's Erotica 2004, 2006* and *2007*, *Best Lesbian Erotica 2009*, *Dirty Girls* and other titles that make her mother blush. Her erotic paranormal romance *Lions' Pride* features a happy nonhuman couple and the hot shapeshifting guy they both love.

THOMAS ROCHE's (thomasroche.com) erotica has appeared in several hundred websites, magazines and anthologies. Earlier books include three volumes in the *Noirotica* series of erotic crime-noir, four anthologies and three collections. A writer of crime, horror, fantasy and science fiction, he is working on a mammoth steampunk murder mystery featuring brain-eating zombies, viruses, rampaging robots and killer mimes.

ALISON TYLER's twenty-five naughty novels and fifty erotic anthologies have won her the title of "Erotica's Own Super Woman" (*East Bay Literary Examiner*). Her most recent collection is *Alison's Wonderland*. Find her 24/7 at alisontyler.blogspot.com.

VANESSA VAUGHN's (VanessaVaughn.com) stories have been included in numerous erotic anthologies from publishers such as Cleis Press, Circlet Press and Ravenous Romance. She believes the best erotica—like the best sex—requires the unexpected, and sometimes even the uncomfortable, to truly satisfy.

ALLISON WONDERLAND (aisforallison.blogspot.com) has contributed to a number of anthologies including *Hurts So Good: Unrestrained Erotica, I Do: An Anthology in Support of Marriage Equality* and *Coming Together: At Last*.

KRISTINA WRIGHT's (kristinawright.com) steamy erotica has appeared in more than seventy anthologies, including *Sweet Life: Erotic Fantasies for Couples* and three editions of *Best Women's Erotica*. She lives in Virginia with her husband and a menagerie of pets and spends a great deal of time writing in coffee shops.

ABOUT THE EDITOR

VIOLET BLUE (tinynibbles.com) is a blogger, high-profile tech personality, award-winning best-selling author and editor of more than two-dozen books in five languages, podcaster, web TV show GETV reporter, technology futurist, and sex-positive pundit in mainstream media (such as CNN and "The Tyra Banks Show"). Violet is the sex columnist for the *San Francisco Chronicle* with a weekly column titled "Open Source Sex" and has a podcast of the same name with more than eight million downloads and counting. Blue is also a Forbes Web Celeb and one of *Wired*'s Faces of Innovation. She writes for media outlets such as *Forbes, O: The Oprah Magazine* and the UN sponsored international health organization, RH Reality Check. Violet lectures to cyberlaw classes at UC Berkeley, human sexuality programs at UCSF, tech conferences (ETech and SXSW), in addition to sex crisis counselors at community teaching institutions and Google Tech Talks. Blue's tech blog is techyum.com and she publishes DRM-free audio and e-books at DigitaPub.com.